"I admit it!" Ethan exploded, ~~her unspoken accusation.~~ *"I just couldn't keep away from you anymore! Even if I'd known you were perfectly safe, even if the fuse hadn't blown, I'd still have found an excuse to see you. I can't take another night of this, Jess!"*

Suddenly the darkness was alive with powerful emotions that seemed to crackle in the air between them like the rattle of a hidden snake. Jess couldn't see Ethan's face, but she heard his desperation, and she stepped back in alarm. She was so used to thinking of him as a man in control of his emotions—patient, reasonable and understanding. But she was suddenly reminded of the man who'd turned on her like a wounded beast the night they'd met.

"Another night of what?" she asked shakily.

"Of wanting you so much I have to spend every hour fighting the urge to break down your door and make love to you. Of wanting so much to convince you that we belong together that I'm tempted to use physical force. It's no use pretending I can fight it much longer—not when you're so close I can hear you turn over in bed at night."

Jess backed a step away from Ethan. "We need to talk, Ethan."

"Let me in, Jess. Let me in," he whispered.

"Ethan, please understand. It's not *you* I don't trust, it's myself!" But his sudden push against the door forced it open a few more inches, and Jess found herself lost in abandon as her lips parted under the fierce hunger of his kiss. . . .

WHAT ARE *LOVESWEPT* ROMANCES?

They are stories of true romance and touching emotion. We believe those two very important ingredients are constants in our highly sensual and very believable stories in the *LOVESWEPT* line. Our goal is to give you, the reader, stories of consistently high quality that may sometimes make you laugh, sometimes make you cry, but are always fresh and creative and contain many delightful surprises within their pages.

Most romance fans read an enormous number of books. Those they truly love, they keep. Others may be traded with friends and soon forgotten. We hope that each *LOVESWEPT* romance will be a treasure—a "keeper." We will always try to publish

LOVE STORIES YOU'LL NEVER FORGET
BY AUTHORS YOU'LL ALWAYS REMEMBER

The Editors

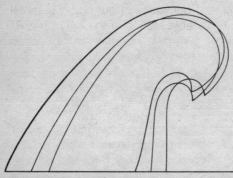

LOVESWEPT · 49

Kathleen Downes
The Man Next Door

BANTAM BOOKS · TORONTO · NEW YORK · LONDON · SYDNEY

THE MAN NEXT DOOR

A Bantam Book / June 1984

*LOVESWEPT and the wave device are trademarks of
Bantam Books, Inc.*

ISBN 0-553-21660-0

Published simultaneously in the United States and Canada

*Bantam Books are published by Bantam Books, Inc. Its trade-
mark, consisting of the words ''Bantam Books'' and the por-
trayal of a rooster, is Registered in U.S. Patent and Trademark
Office and in other countries. Marca Registrada. Bantam
Books, Inc., 666 Fifth Avenue, New York, New York 10103.*

PRINTED IN THE UNITED STATES OF AMERICA

O   0 9 8 7 6 5 4 3 2 1

One

Jess became aware of the angry voices next door as she turned off the spray that had been drumming against the shower stall in accompaniment to her own exuberant but off-key rendition of an old Beatles tune. The walls in the little duplex cabin were certainly thin, but until now she hadn't realized just *how* thin. The previous occupants of the adjacent unit had been a retired couple on an annual fishing holiday. They'd been coming to plain, unpretentious Bill's Cabins on the Mendocino coast of California for twenty years, they told Jess. And they had made less noise in a week than the new couple had made in the past five minutes.

"All I can say is you've got a lot of nerve bringing me to a dump like this!" a woman's voice snapped.

"Beryl, please, just give it a chance." The man's deep tones attempted to be soothing, but a thread of barely controlled impatience was evident. "Wait till you see the view on a sunny day. Then you'll understand why I love this place. It's got a character all its own."

"Character! That's about *all* it's got, Ethan. No TV, no restaurant, no bar, no pool, no golf course, no interesting people to meet. Just dampness and fog and smelly fishermen, and weird females like that would-be artist who gave you the eye when we checked in. And now some tone-deaf moron who sings in the shower!"

Weird female! Tone-deaf moron! Jess went hot with anger and embarrassment, and then gave a rueful laugh. She quickly toweled herself dry and scrambled into jeans and a sweater. Well, she admitted, she did feel a bit of a fool to have been heard singing her heart out with such abandon, especially now that she realized who the two next door were. She'd seen them checking in that afternoon, and the note of cold disdain in the woman's voice corresponded exactly to the expression the tall, ice-cool blonde had worn earlier as she gingerly descended the old wooden steps on her spike heels.

From the minute Jess had glanced up from her easel that afternoon, she'd felt antagonism toward the couple. The man's beautifully cut wool business suit indicated to her knowing eye that he had driven here directly from a San Francisco office, and everything about him proclaimed that that office was in the executive suite at a fancy address and had plush carpets, expensive wooden furniture, and, no doubt, a stunning view of the bay. He didn't belong here. So it was odd that the look on his lean, hard-angled face seemed to be one of approval as he scanned the half dozen shabby little duplex cabins scattered across the grassy headland, with the old wooden water tower looming above them in the late-afternoon fog.

It was true that Jess had stared at him, but she certainly hadn't been "giving him the eye" in the crude sexual sense the blonde implied. No, indeed. The last thing she needed was to get mixed up with another ambition-driven, success-dominated, money-fixated male, and that was exactly what this man appeared to be, from the expensively casual cut of his dark hair right down the full six-foot-plus length of him to his costly leather shoes. And as if that weren't enough to warn her away, there was even a hint of uncanny resemblance to Cliff in the aggressive angle of his jaw and the set of his broad shoulders.

She was surprised, now, to learn that they'd even noticed her tucked behind her easel in an out-of-the-way corner. In her windblown, paint-spattered condition she'd felt downright invisible, next to their immaculate sophistication. No wonder the blonde had referred to her as a "weird female." But it was the term "would-be artist" that really rankled. There was no "would-be" about it—she *was* an artist! Jess hadn't yet made a big name for herself, but at the age of twenty-seven, after years of hard work and almost single-minded dedication to painting, she knew what she was and what she could do.

The voices next door invaded her consciousness once more, and now it seemed that the man's persuasive tones were carrying the day.

"Please put up with it for a few days, Beryl. I've got a sentimental attachment to the place. Did I tell you my family used to come here when I was a kid?"

"Yes, and I'll bet nobody's replaced a stick of furniture since then!" But this time Beryl didn't sound genuinely angry. A reluctant little smile had crept into her voice. Then she actually giggled. "You probably slept on this very mattress! Perhaps on these very sheets!"

"For your information, I was probably *conceived* on these very sheets!" the man drawled wickedly, and the bedsprings creaked alarmingly as another burst of giggles erupted.

The next few nights could prove very nerve-racking if she had to listen to this sort of thing, Jess thought indignantly. She made a great racket with the pots and pans as she set about preparing her supper, trying to shut out the sounds of any lovemaking that might be taking place. Her precautions were apparently unnecessary, however, for almost immediately there were sounds of suitcases opening and Beryl's voice calling, "Have you seen my shampoo, Ethan?"

"Put a robe on, for God's sake, or we'll never get out of here before the restaurants close!" his voice rasped in answer.

Jess heard another giggle, and then the slam of the bathroom door. The shower was turned on full force for several minutes, and Jess forgot about the couple next door while she concentrated on cutting up the onions and potatoes for the fish chowder she was making. And then came an ear-splitting scream.

"Beryl! Are you all right?" The whole cabin shook as the man charged across the floor and flung open the bathroom door.

"It's cold! The water went ice-cold on me!" Beryl shrieked, and Jess, who had almost sliced off a finger in shock, sighed with relief and impatience.

"Is that all? I forgot to tell you they have a chronic water shortage here, so they like to discourage long showers. The hot water tanks don't hold much, and that songbird next door must have used up most of it," the man explained.

"So what am I supposed to do?" Beryl wailed. "My hair is all soaped up! This is all your fault! You should have warned me!"

"I'm sorry. I forgot. Why don't you just give it a quick rinse? A little cold water won't hurt you."

"I'll never forgive you for this, Ethan." The bathroom door slammed. The cold-water rinse that followed was brief indeed, and then Beryl's extreme displeasure was conveyed by the sound of her angry footsteps and the loud thuds with which she rummaged through her suitcase. "Where can I plug this in?" she asked at last in an icy voice.

"Uh . . . I don't think that's a good idea. You see—"

"I don't give a damn what you think. I'm going to dry my hair."

Oh, no! Jess looked around wildly for her flashlight, spotted it on the table by her bed, and made a headlong dash across the room.

"Beryl, wait!" But obviously Beryl didn't wait, for the whine of the portable electric hair dryer was abruptly silenced as the room plunged into total darkness. Jess sighed, and switched on her flash-light. By its beam she made quick work of lighting the old-fashioned oil lamp that graced the kitchen table. She remembered thinking a week ago, when she first arrived, that the old lamp added a quaint touch to an otherwise utilitarian room, but she'd quickly learned it was a far from frivolous addition to the decor. The wiring in the old cabin was quite inadequate, and the least thing was likely to blow a fuse.

Just then the man let off a string of angry curses that made Jess very glad not to be Beryl right now. "Wouldn't you know I left the flashlight in the car?" he asked finally. "Where the hell are those matches?" Various muffled thuds and clangs indicated that he was searching for them quite vigorously. At last Jess heard the rasp and flare as he struck a match.

"Cheer up, Beryl," he said. "I'll get this lamp lit and then see about replacing the fuse. We'll have the power back on in no time."

"Don't bother. I'm not staying here another minute."

"Come on, Beryl. Be reasonable."

"*Reasonable*? You bring me to this sleazy place, where I can't even take a shower or dry my hair, and then you ask *me* to be reasonable!" Beryl's control had broken, and her voice climbed hysterically and went on and on, pouring out grievances.

"With all your piles of money, Ethan, we could have gone *anywhere*! You could have taken me cruis-ing in the Caribbean or shopping in Paris! If you simply *had* to spend a week up here on this misera-ble coast, at least you could have taken me to a decent resort. I thought you cared about me, Ethan, but now I see exactly how you really feel! I'm not good enough for fancy hotels and mixing with impor-tant people, am I? Oh, no, I'm the girl you take to a cheap old shack in the middle of nowhere!"

"That's not true." His voice sounded incredibly weary, drained of all energy. "Listen, we're both tired and hungry. Let's have something to eat, then get a good night's sleep. We'll talk in the morning."

"I refuse to stay here tonight!"

"I'm not going to quarrel anymore, Beryl. Excuse me while I take a shower—the colder the better. We'll leave for the restaurant in ten minutes."

"You can't order me around like one of your damn employees, Ethan!" There was no response except the slamming of the bathroom door.

Jess found herself gripping the edge of the kitchen counter, conscious of a sick feeling in her stomach. The earlier squabbles had seemed amusing, but there was nothing funny about Beryl's pathetic tirade and Ethan's tired, despairing voice. Jess had been through enough bitter lovers' quarrels of her own—she had no desire to listen to anyone else's.

But she couldn't block out the sounds from next door. Ethan was obviously in the shower now, and Beryl must be dressed, if the click of high heels was any indication. Suitcases were snapped shut and dragged across the floor to the accompaniment of the clicking heels. The door opened, the door shut, and the dragging suitcases and angry footsteps proceeded up the wooden steps and along the plank walk toward the parking lot.

When Ethan turned off the shower, there was only the sound of far-off waves crashing on the rocky cliffs below the headlands. Finally came the roar of a starting engine and the loud spinning of tires as a furious driver accelerated onto the gravel road that led away from the quiet isolation of Bill's Cabins, back to the highways and motels and neon lights.

It was horrible to listen to the sounds of the man's gradual realization that Beryl had run out on him. The calling of her name, the dashing out to the parking lot, the silent return, the sudden crash as some object was hurled against the wall, the clinking of a glass as he poured himself a drink, and then the utter silence save for the distant sound of the breaking waves—all of it was horrible.

Jess huddled in a rickety wooden chair, her arms resting on the table and her fists pressed against her temples. It was none of her business, and heaven knew she didn't want to get involved. Still, how could she let another human being suffer alone on the other side of that wall without lifting a finger to help him even though she had disliked him on sight? Yet what could she say to him? Impossible to confess that she'd been eavesdropping the whole time, but what conceivable excuse could she make for barging in on a perfect stranger? He wouldn't thank her for her concern, in any case. He'd probably throw something at *her*. No, he was better off left alone.

On the gas stove the fish chowder simmered, redolent of butter, garlic, cream, and freshly caught fish—a parting gift from her former neighbors, who'd checked out that morning. There was a crusty, fragrant loaf of sourdough bread to go with it, purchased at a bakery in the nearby village of Mendocino that morning to turn this meal into a miniature feast. It was supposed to be a reward for a week of virtuous daily jogging and light meals as Jess tried to shed a few unwelcome pounds. At this moment she felt she never wanted to eat again. Had the man next door lost his appetite too? He'd said he was hungry, but now he didn't even have a way to get out to a restaurant, assuming he and Beryl had driven up together.

It would be simple enough to offer him a meal. No need to search for words of comfort for a man with whom she had nothing in common and who would no doubt resent her pity. She'd just give him something to eat. After all, she couldn't leave him to starve. And she couldn't leave him alone with his troubles, because if he did something desperate— though he hardly seemed the type—she'd never forgive herself.

It took five minutes to work up the courage to venture out the door. Nervously she tried to smooth the unruly tendrils of honey-brown hair that always escaped from the single thick braid that hung to her waist. The moisture from the shower had made every loose strand curl riotously. The curls clustered untidily to frame her piquant, lightly freckled face.

Already she felt at a disadvantage, facing a man accustomed to the soignée elegance of women like Beryl, a man who was himself composed of such clean, strong, simple lines that he would never look untidy even if clothed in rags. But it was ridiculous to stand here worrying about her appearance. Resolutely she opened the door and marched briskly along the plank walk to where that other door waited forbiddingly.

If she stopped to think, she was lost, so she knocked on the door and fixed a bright, fragile smile on her lips.

"What do you want?" the deep, familiar voice barked at her as the door opened a crack.

"Hello!" she began in a brittle cheery tone that sounded jarringly false even to her own ears. "I'm Jess Winslow, your neighbor from the other side of the wall. I just thought I'd drop by to welcome you to Bill's and offer you some homemade fish chowder if you're hungry."

"No. I'm not hungry." He moved to shut the door, and, without stopping to think, Jess thrust her foot into the crack.

"Wait! I *know* you must be hungry, and you're stranded here without a car at least till morning. It's crazy to sit and drink all night without getting some food into your system." The shock of his outright refusal had stampeded her into the revealing outburst. It was a foolish mistake. There was a moment's pause as the implications of her words sank in, and then the explosion came.

"Hell!" The door was flung open, and brutally strong hands seized her by the arms and yanked her into the room, slamming the door shut behind her. "You snooping, prying, interfering bitch. I suppose you've been listening the whole damn time?"

"I couldn't help . . ." Jess gulped in panic. She couldn't have said which terrified her most: the savage violence in his face, the iron grip of his hands, or the fact that he wore nothing but a brief terry-cloth robe. And then there were his eyes. Their tawny golden color was unusual, but the real shock was in the tiny dark lines that radiated in a sunburst pattern round his pupils. Tiger eyes! And at the moment they glittered with untamed rage.

"So you couldn't wait to offer your services to the poor, lonely, *rich* bachelor, could you? You're a regular angel of mercy! Swooping down like a vulture to take your pickings."

"Now, just a minute!" A shaft of pure rage shot through her, and she struggled furiously to escape his grasp. Abruptly he jerked her against his chest and held her imprisoned there. For a second there was no sound but their rapid heartbeats, hers fluttering like the pulse of a terrified bird. Her senses took irrelevant note of the soap-scented dampness of the wiry curls on his chest where her face was forced against his flesh. A part of her was also conscious of the pressure of his lean, muscular thighs.

"Since you're so eager to give me aid and comfort, perhaps you'd care to demonstrate just what you have to offer?" he jeered. "I'm not in the mood for fish chowder."

Roughly he forced her chin up and enveloped her mouth with his. Though she clenched her teeth against him, her lips were most persuasively plundered for his scornful appraisal, and then his tongue ran silkenly along the closed wall of her teeth and the rosy flesh of her gums. His implacable hands moved in maddeningly intimate caresses across her hips, breasts, and waist, scarcely deterred by her efforts to free herself.

His onslaught had jolted her brain into temporary paralysis. She couldn't cope with the shock waves of fear and anger that hammered through her nervous system, their very intensity leaving her numb. This simply couldn't be happening.

And then came a tiny rush of feeling that was neither rage nor panic. It was desire, trickling hot and treacherously sweet at the very heart of her. Ethan's tongue had suddenly breached the defenses of her mouth, plunging into the warm, soft depths to claim possession there. And simultaneously his hand tunneled beneath her sweater and climbed the peak of her breast.

Oddly enough, the knowledge that she was being sexually aroused against her will was what impelled Jess to regain control. Suddenly her brain was working again, quite coolly and rationally, telling her that she couldn't allow this to continue. This man's violent, contemptuous assault must not be permitted to succeed to *any* extent. She forced herself to go limp against his heated flesh, her weight throwing him off-balance for the fraction of a second she needed to undertake her all-or-nothing attempt to break his hold.

It worked. Using every iota of speed and strength she possessed, Jess tore herself out of his arms and leaped across the room, putting the kitchen table between herself and him. She would have preferred to be safely out his door, but she hadn't dared try to escape that way, for it would take only an instant of fumbling at the doorknob, with her back turned to him, for her advantage to be lost. At least this way, facing him, she didn't feel so utterly helpless.

He moved toward her, breathing heavily, and her hands seized on the first object they encountered on the stove top behind her—a small, cast-iron skillet.

"Stop this craziness! Stop it!" she cried as she brandished the makeshift weapon.

He took another step toward her and then stopped dead, blinking like a man suddenly wakened from a dream. He stared at her in bafflement, as if wondering how this could possibly be happening. Why was he advancing like a beast of prey about to spring on a total stranger who clutched a frying pan in her trembling hand and eyed him as if she expected to have to fight for her life at any second?

"You won't be needing that frying pan," he said at last, and his voice was weary once more, but threaded with amusement. "I may have gotten carried away, but not *that* carried away." Cautiously Jess lowered the skillet, waiting for his apology. Instead he said,

"Next time you'll know better than to go looking for trouble."

Jess tried to keep her voice level, but it pulsated with the vehemence of her anger. "Listen, you conceited fool, I didn't come here asking to be mauled by you. For your information, I haven't the slightest interest in you or your money. I was only trying to help a fellow human being, regardless of age, sex, creed, color, *or income.* My conscience would have bothered me if I hadn't tried to make sure that at the very least you didn't go hungry."

He leaned toward her across the table, and the intensity of his golden, probing stare made her shiver. He spoke softly and deliberately.

"In the midst of all your good intentions, did it never once occur to you that a man in my situation just might want to be left alone? That privacy might be the best thing you could give him? But no, you had to come picking and prying, didn't you?"

"If you wanted privacy, you should have said so, instead of manhandling me. All I did was offer you a meal! How was I to guess you'd actually prefer to sit here starving yourself and wallowing in self-pity?" Immediately the words were spoken, she wished them unsaid. He had reason to feel miserable, after all. "I'm sorry," she muttered.

"Well, now that you've so virtuously done your duty, Miss—"

"Winslow. Jessica Winslow," she said miserably. He had succeeded in making her feel like a meddling busybody. "I'm sorry for the intrusion, and now I'll leave you in peace. Good night." She scuttled across the floor, aching with humiliation.

"Good night, Miss Winslow," she heard him say just as she plunged out the door into the welcome darkness.

Alone in her room, she sank down on the bed, trembling. She had been so very afraid, and so angry, and then so embarrassed. Now she felt an uneasy mixture of all three emotions. When she tried to close her eyes, her mind filled with the image of the man's furious, mocking, unhappy face, crowned by rumpled dark hair. Her limbs still felt the aftershock of his harsh embrace, which had left a tingling vulnerability that frightened her. She didn't want to feel vulnerable to *him.*

Anything would be better than lying here thinking such thoughts, so Jess picked up her flashlight and went outside to replace the blown fuse. She took the last fuse from the cardboard carton perched atop the fuse box, and made a mental note to ask Bill or Ann Jenkins, the owners, for a new supply. After shutting off the current, she quickly unscrewed the blasted fuse and twisted the new one into place. With a pull of the lever, power was restored and light came spilling out the cabin windows in bright rectangular patterns along the ground.

Back inside, Jess bustled about reheating the lukewarm chowder and setting the table. She refused to think about the recent unpleasant incident. After dinner, she would work on sketching until she was ready to drop from exhaustion, and only then would she try to get some sleep. Just as she decided this, there was a knock on the door. An irrational wave of panic swept through her, and she stood staring at the door in silent hope that the menace would simply go away.

"Miss Winslow?" It was the voice she'd been fearing. "This is Ethan Jamieson, your neighbor. Thanks for changing the fuse."

"That's quite all right." Now go away, she begged silently.

"I've come to apologize. Won't you open the door? I promise I'll behave myself. Please. I feel damn silly talking to a plank of wood."

Jess knew all the rules for a woman living alone—rules like not opening the door to strangers. And especially not to a large, unpredictable male stranger who had already shown himself to be capable of violence. But it wasn't violence that she feared from Ethan Jamieson. In fact, she wasn't quite sure *what* it was about him that made her feel threatened. But she had to find out, because Jess was in the habit of confronting her fears head-on, not hiding from them. So now she had to open that door to find out why she was afraid of a man with tiger-striped eyes.

Two

Jess was not about to throw all caution to the wind, however. She opened the door only a crack, and peered out warily. A bar of light fell through the opening and illuminated the man's face. It was transformed by a good-humored, almost boyish sheepishness. Fully clothed in jeans and bulky sweater, Ethan Jamieson was much less alarming than the half-naked man she'd so recently confronted. And his eyes, for the moment, were only striped, pussy-cat eyes.

"I'm sorry about the way I acted earlier," he said earnestly. "It was really very decent of you to be concerned about me, and you certainly didn't deserve the reception you got. I'm afraid I was feeling a bit raw, and I just lashed out blindly at the first person to come along. Unfortunately that happened to be you."

"I understand. Your apology is accepted, Mr. Jamieson." On that note of cool formality she moved to shut the door, to lock out the man's disturbing, forceful presence.

It was not to be. His foot was as suddenly and firmly planted in the doorway as her own foot had impulsively blocked *his* closing door less than an hour ago.

"Call me Ethan. And won't you please take pity again on a starving man? I don't know what possessed me to refuse your earlier generous offer of dinner, but the truth is I'm hungry as a bear. And as you yourself pointed out, I'm stranded here without my car."

Jess hesitated. She didn't want to share a meal with this man, yet how could she turn him away after such an appeal? And wouldn't that be like giving in to a cowardly impulse? She couldn't let fear get the better of her. But still she hesitated.

"Don't worry. I'm usually quite harmless. Look, I even brought some peace offerings," he added coaxingly, holding up a bottle of wine. Jess found herself opening the door just a little wider and reaching for the chilled bottle. When he placed it in her hands, she discovered it was slippery with condensed moisture, and she might have dropped it if the man hadn't instantly stepped in and caught it neatly with one hand as it was sliding out of her grasp. His sudden nearness and his amused smile set her nerves to clamoring.

He was holding something else, hidden behind his back, and for one monstrous irrational instant all Jess's fears rose up inside her and she imagined it might be a weapon. His apology had been a clever ruse, and now he meant to . . .

"May I put this in your freezer until we're ready for dessert?" he asked, holding out a pint-sized container of chocolate–macadamia nut ice cream.

Jess stared at it for a second as if it were a scorpion, and then something inside her seemed to give way and she found herself laughing. At first her laughter was shaky and slightly hysterical, but it mellowed to a deep, genuine, cleansing relief of tension. "How did you guess?" she asked, trying to catch her breath.

"What? That you love ice cream? Or that this is your favorite flavor?"

"Both!"

"Oh, I can always spot a fellow ice-cream addict—it's a sixth sense I have, since I'm always looking for partners in crime. As for the flavor, that was a lucky coincidence, since chocolate–macadamia nut happens to be my favorite as well."

"So we actually have something in common?"

"Don't sound so surprised!"

But she *was* surprised. It was nice to know that even though he looked like the type who might read *The Wall Street Journal* for fun, he still had his priorities right about something. Yes, even though he was so stuck on himself and his financial success that he assumed every woman must be after him, his enthusiasm for ice cream was quite . . . endearing. Maybe he wasn't such a bad guy after all.

It was at that moment that Ethan noticed her paintings, several of which were propped against walls and furniture around the tiny room. Jess sensed a sudden alertness about him. He was like a jungle cat on the trail of a fresh scent.

But Jess didn't want him pouncing on her paintings. She remembered what an ordeal it always had been to show her work to Cliff. Even though he wasn't terribly interested and knew next to nothing about art, Cliff was the sort of man who always had to express an opinion about everything. That was one of his techniques for projecting the right image of authority and success—he would state his views, without hesitation, on any subject whatsoever, as if he were an expert in that field. Never mind that Jess was a professional artist—Cliff had proceeded to lecture her on how she'd never amount to anything if she didn't paint pictures that *he* could understand. He'd never been able to grasp the idea that art, like music, was an intensely personal expression of something that went beyond words, beyond simple explanations.

Her experiences with Cliff had left Jess with a king-sized prejudice against the kind of man who moved in the elite circles of the high-powered business world. The process of clawing his way to the top had molded Cliff so that all he thought about was making money and manipulating people. And his friends were just like him. Their minds all worked the same way.

Jess had no intention ever again of letting someone with those attitudes try to tell her about her own paintings. And if her first impressions of Ethan Jamieson were correct, he was precisely that sort of man.

"Did you do these?" he asked now, and Jess nodded. "Do you mind if I have a look?"

"Be my guest. But please don't tell me what you think of them, because frankly—"

"Frankly, my deah, I don't give a damn," he chimed in with the old Clark Gable line. "Was that what you meant to say?"

"Well, more or less. In fact, yes."

"Fair enough." There was a pucker of laughter around his mouth.

"Unless you consider yourself an expert?"

"Not at all." He went around the room in silence, carefully studying her paintings. His expression gave nothing away, and Jess found herself contrarily wishing he'd betray at least some reaction. But he said nothing at all until they sat down to bowls of steaming chowder.

"This smells marvelous!" he exclaimed, and Jess watched in gratified amusement as he savored the first spoonful. "I do consider myself something of an expert about *food*," he said. "And this meal calls for a toast." He raised his glass of wine. "To a good Samaritan who can cook!"

"To a penitent who comes bearing chocolate—macadamia nut ice cream!" Jess responded, laughing, and they clinked glasses with great gusto. The cupboard hadn't yielded any wineglasses, so they were making do with jelly jars, but Jess thought even the finest crystal couldn't have added to the suddenly festive mood that sprang up between them.

There was an air of suppressed excitement about Ethan now, a current of energy that seemed to leap from his tiger-striped eyes straight to Jess. She couldn't deny that he was very entertaining. Their conversation bounded from one topic to another with a playful exuberance that Jess found uniquely stimulating.

In no time at all they'd established that they both lived and worked in San Francisco, and Jess secretly congratulated herself that at least part of her hunch about him was confirmed. But she soon forgot all her preconceived notions of his character as they talked. Books, movies, politics, lifestyles, and, of course, food—each subject provided grounds for animated argument or agreement. Ethan's comments were never predictable, and he seemed eager to hear Jess's ideas, giving them the same zestful attention that he bestowed on each bite of his meal.

By the time the wine bottle and chowder pot were empty and the bread had been reduced to a few crumbs, Jess felt as if she'd known Ethan for years. Except that she knew nothing of his work or of his personal life. As if by unspoken agreement, they had avoided asking those questions or volunteering that information.

So it was something of a shock when Ethan suddenly said, "Now tell me about your paintings."

"What do you want to know?" Jess asked lightly, trying to hold on to her effervescent mood.

"Everything. To start with, which galleries show your work, and what kind of prices do you charge?"

Jess felt as if she'd been slapped. How dare he pretend genuine interest in her work when his questions showed that her creations were nothing to him but economic commodities to be bought and sold! But what the hell had she expected from a guy who showed up at Bill's Cabins wearing a three-piece suit? Of course his first thought was money. Of course he had a businessman's mentality that looked at art as just another possible "investment." She'd suspected all that from the first. So why did she feel this sense of personal betrayal? Had she begun to hope that he might be different, just because he liked chocolate–macadamia nut ice cream, because his dinner conversation sparkled with wit, and because he possessed the most beguiling smile she'd ever seen in her life? Well, now she knew better.

Some of her displeasure must have shown, for Ethan asked quickly, "They *are* for sale, aren't they? Surely you don't paint like this just as a hobby?"

Hobby. Cliff had called it that once, with a sneer in his voice, during one of their final, painful confrontations.

"No, painting is my profession," Jess said coldly. In calm, businesslike tones, she told him the typical price she charged for one of her paintings, and mentioned the name of a small, little-known gallery that occasionally carried some of her work.

"How do you manage to make a living at it, if you don't mind my asking?"

Of course she minded. This man, with his mind like a computer, programmed for financial success, would never understand why anything as financially unrewarding as painting was so important to her. Nor would he understand why she'd been willing to make the financial sacrifices she had. Nor was it any of his business. But he was gazing at her with intent, curious, brown-and-gold eyes that seemed to compel an answer.

"I *don't* make a living at it—not yet," she answered quietly. "I hope someday my paintings will bring in enough money to pay the bills, but for now I support myself doing secretarial work on the side, for a temporary agency. The pay's not great, but working as a temp gives me flexibility. There's no long-term commitment to a job, so my work at the office isn't likely to preoccupy me or spill over to interfere with my painting."

"Still, it must be a strain to find enough energy and creative drive for painting after a day at the typewriter."

"It's not so different from what thousands of other women do. They work all day because they have to, but when they get home they manage to find the energy to do the things they do for love, like taking care of their families."

"But there *is* a difference," he protested, and Jess was surprised by his seriousness. "Your love of painting can't take the place of human relationships, so you not only have to make a living *and* do the emotionally demanding work of an artist, but then you also have to make time for the people in your life. Surely the juggling act must get a little exhausting sometimes."

"Of course it does," Jess answered, smiling wryly. In fact, the "juggling act" could become downright impossible, as it had several months ago, when she'd realized that Cliff would never respect the seriousness of her commitment to painting. It had hurt to let that part of her life hit the ground with a large crash, but it hadn't taken her long to discover that only her engagement was broken, after all—not her heart.

Ethan was watching her as if he expected her to share these thoughts with him, but Jess had no intention of doing so. Yet she'd better start talking about *something.*

"It's important for me to be able to get away for a holiday like this, where all I have to do is paint," she quickly informed him. "It's such a relief to focus on that and nothing else. That's the good thing about working for Bon Temps Agency—yes, isn't that name the most ghastly pun you ever heard?" She laughingly acknowledged his incredulous stare. "Working as a temp, I don't have to worry about leaving some employer in the lurch when I go on vacation."

"What about your other relationships? Are they temporary too? Or don't you worry about leaving a boyfriend in the lurch?" His tone was casual and amused, but the dark-spoked, tawny eyes were narrowed in a way that made Jess suddenly uneasy.

"I think I've answered enough questions for now, Mr. Jamieson," she said abruptly. Quickly she stood up and began collecting the dishes, reaching across the width of the table to avoid stepping close to him.

Her hand was just stretching out to remove his empty wineglass when Ethan lightly imprisoned her wrist between his thumb and forefinger. His touch sent twin jolts of fear and sensual awareness quivering through her. Hastily she tried to snatch her hand away, but the gentle pressure of his fingers was as strong as a steel manacle, holding her captive.

Furiously, her birch-green eyes met his golden ones. Their faces were less than a foot apart, and Jess felt exposed and vulnerable in the awkward position she'd been forced into. Leaning across the table like this, she was conscious of her breasts dangling ripely before him, and she knew that his eyes savored the weight and fullness of them, and traced the outlines of her taut nipples, with an almost tactile intensity.

Living Technicolor urges invaded her brain. Her face flushed to a dusky rose color, and Jess was furious with both herself and Ethan Jamieson, more at herself for permitting erotic fantasies to overwhelm her.

"Please let go of me, Mr. Jamieson."

"Of course, *Miss Winslow,*" he murmured, while his intimately searching eyes and silkenly caressing tone made a mockery of her brisk attempt at formality. And then, with one last sensuous stroke of his thumb across her pulse, he let her go. Nothing had happened.

With rapidly beating heart, Jess turned around and moved to the sink. She was trembling as she ran hot water over the dishes. Damn her vivid imagination anyway! As an artist, her ability to visualize a scene down to the last detail was a helpful tool, but as a woman trying to hide her unwelcome sexual response to a man she disapproved of, it was a definite drawback. She hoped Ethan hadn't guessed the erotic picture of seduction her fantasy had painted.

"I wasn't asking about the other men in your life out of idle curiosity, you know." His deep-timbred voice suddenly spoke from only a few inches behind her, and Jess felt her fragile composure shatter into little pieces. Everything was getting out of control. How could she deal with her own outrageous physical reaction to this man if he started getting amorous ideas of his own?

The whole situation was ridiculous. Only a few hours ago they'd never even met, and Ethan had still been expecting to spend the night with Beryl! He was practically a stranger. And he was exactly the kind of man she'd sworn to steer clear of after her disastrous relationship with Cliff. They had only one ridiculous thing in common: a fondness for ice cream.

The only thing to do was pretend it wasn't happening. Pretend his question hadn't meant a thing. Pretend that his warm breath stirring the tendrils of hair on her neck didn't send ripples of pleasure down her spine. All it required was a little willpower. She simply had to iron some starch into her voice and then put him at a distance and keep him there.

"Idle or not, I'm tired of answering your questions," she snapped, flinging him an antagonistic look over her shoulder. "In fact, why don't you do some talking about *yourself*, for a change? You could tell me where you made that pile of money you're so proud of. Was it in high finance? Real estate? Corporate management?"

"Nothing so glamorous, I'm afraid." Jess glanced at him again and saw that he wasn't sure how to take her hostile mood. He seemed half-amused, half-puzzled.

"So what was it?" she asked. "Drug smuggling? Funeral parlors?"

"No, of course not." He laughed. "I work in the food retailing business. I specialize in promotional R & D."

"R & D?"

"Research and development."

"I see," said Jess, though she didn't see at all. "I suppose you're one of those geniuses who invents ways to make TV dinners out of polyester, and breakfast cereals out of sugared cardboard?" Surely he'd take offense at *that* and stop looking so damned amused.

"Not exactly," he answered, trying not to laugh.

"Of course. I forgot you said you were in *promotional* R & D. Your job must be to convince the public to buy the artificial concoctions that come out of the chemistry labs."

"Why are you so determined to misunderstand me?" he asked, but his eyes still glinted with humor rather than anger. "I refuse to say one more word about my job, since you're obviously all set to poke fun at it, no matter what it is. Besides, if you get me started talking about my work, I'll go on for hours. I love what I do, but it has a tendency to take over too much of my life if I let it. And this is supposed to be my vacation."

So he was a self-confessed workaholic. Jess wasn't in the least surprised. It was all part of the pattern.

"Let's forget about work," he went on. "I want to concentrate on you." And then he took her by the waist and drew her back against his lean frame, so that her gently rounded, denim-clad posterior nestled against his muscular thighs. His arms wrapped themselves round her midriff, and his words were like sibilant kisses against her ear. "I need to know, Jessica Winslow, if there's a man in your life you want to be faithful to, or are you free?"

"Free?" she echoed, dazed by the tumult of longing that his hard body aroused in her. So much for willpower.

"Free to get involved with me," he whispered, kissing her earlobe and then brushing his lips along the curve of her neck. One hand moved up to fondle the tips of her breasts, while the other moved in leisurely strokes along her taut stomach.

Jess fought the urge to surrender, simply to accept the tide of exquisite sensation that washed over her. This was all wrong—she and this man were hopelessly mismatched. There could be no chance of a satisfying relationship between them, except in the most basic physical sense. And a purely sexual liaison was such an empty thing—like a fire without warmth.

He turned her in his arms, and Jess knew that she had to stop him before he kissed her.

"No. I'm not free," she cried, pushing him away. His face was suddenly grim and still, except for his glittering, savage eyes. "It's not what you think," she said quickly. "There *is* someone I want to be faithful to, but it's not some man—it's myself."

"What are you talking about?"

"I'm talking about my self-respect! May I remind you that you arrived in Mendocino with another woman, expecting to make love to *her* tonight? But she left you stranded, so now you think you can just waltz next door and find a replacement before bedtime! Well, I am *not* available."

"When you put it like that, it does sound rather . . . rather shallow," he admitted. "But—"

"It sounds completely tacky!" she exclaimed. "And how else *could* you put it? Facts are facts."

"Yes, but my version of the facts is a bit different. The first fact is that I didn't just 'waltz' over here; you invited me. I wasn't in the mood for company, but I needed a meal, so I came. And then something rather unexpected happened. The lady next door turned out to be somebody special—so special that I completely forgot how I happened to wind up eating her chowder, until she reminded me just now."

"Save it for someone who *likes* cow manure, Mr. Jamieson. I don't happen to have a shovel handy."

"You doubt my sincerity?" His look of amused reproach made Jess want to gnash her teeth. "Tell me, don't you believe in love at first sight?"

"*No.*"

"Neither do I. It certainly didn't happen at *first* sight." He had the gall to grin. "Nor even at the second or third, for that matter. But somehow, after less than an hour in the lady's company, I knew we'd be spending a long, long time together."

"Pardon me if I'm not flattered. It didn't take me nearly that long to decide that you weren't even my type. So I'm afraid we won't be spending much time together after all, Mr. Jamieson."

"Is that so?" The tiger-striped eyes were narrowed again. "Somehow I got the impression that I might be very *much* your type. You're not terribly good at hiding what happens inside that delectable body of yours every time I touch you, you know."

"How dare you be so insulting?" So he had guessed. She had given herself away. Damn!

"Facts are facts, as you once said to me." He shrugged in an infuriating way. "Even as angry as I was when you came knocking at my door, I couldn't help noticing that your kisses packed quite a wallop. Don't try to deny that we're generating some pretty high-voltage electricity here."

"Then maybe it's time you left. I'd hate to overload the circuits." Her voice dripped with sarcasm, but Jess was frightened. If he knew how powerful the mutual attraction was, then he must also guess how dangerously thin the protective shell of her resistance was. All it would take was one long, hard, fiery kiss, and all her defenses would crumble. Scruples, principles, and just plain common sense would be swept away by the violent surge of her inner storm.

"I'll leave when I've had everything I'm entitled to." He took a step toward her, and Jess backed away in panic. His eyes gleamed with predatory mischief.

"And just what do you think you're entitled to?" she hissed as she retreated right up against the door of the refrigerator. Ethan followed.

"Dessert," he whispered, reaching out to seize her by the shoulders.

"No!" she cried, struggling like a wild animal in his grasp. But he merely picked her up and set her aside while he opened the refrigerator door and reached into the freezer compartment.

"Why the big fuss? Don't you want to share the ice

cream?" His phony look of exaggerated disappointment was threatened by the laughter that twitched at the corners of his mouth. Ethan was obviously very pleased with his own cleverness.

"You . . . you rat!" Jess could scarcely spit the words out. "You deliberately set me up. You played on my fears with your John Wayne act just so you could *laugh* at me! Well, congratulations. I hope you're proud of yourself." To her horror, her voice began to shake, and she felt hot, bitter tears of anger sliding down her face. The final straw.

But Ethan didn't seem inclined to gloat over her humiliation. His look of abject dismay would have been comical, if Jess had been in the mood for humor.

"Wait—Don't—I didn't mean—It was just a joke, for crying out loud!" And suddenly Jess felt herself pressed very hard against Ethan's chest, while his large hands stroked soothingly across her shoulders. She held herself rigid, determined not to be softened by the gesture. "I wasn't trying to make fun of *you*," Ethan said with his lips against her honey-brown hair.

"Tell me another one," Jess muttered bitterly.

"It's true. You know what they say about jokes—that we sometimes use them to express the feelings that we're afraid to acknowledge openly. Humor is a way of releasing our tensions, because it allows us to bring our secret fears and desires out into the open, though in a disguised form."

"Thanks for the insight, Dr. Freud, but what does that have to do with the nasty little trick you played on me?"

"Can't you guess? I think it was a way of acting out my impulses without being as selfish as I wanted to be. You see, I know you want me." Jess trembled to hear him say it so matter-of-factly. "But I also know that you don't *want* to want me. Obviously the quickest way to convince you would be to rush in and overwhelm your defenses, using caveman tactics. But I don't happen to have much respect for that approach. Sure, some women prefer it, because they don't like taking responsibility for their own decisions. But you're no coward, and I don't have any right to *force* you to choose me for your lover."

"I should say not!"

"But I know I *could*, you see. And for once I feel mighty tempted to do just that and let my principles go to blazes. So that's what the joke was all about—I was dealing with that temptation in what I thought was a harmless manner."

"Thanks for nothing! I never heard anything so conceited in my life. You have a rather inflated opinion of your attractiveness, Mr. Jamieson."

"Don't you think it might be wise to drop the insults and challenges for a while? That is, unless you *want* to escalate the sexual tension between us right back up to where it was before my attempt at humor cooled things down?" His warning was clear.

Jess admitted to herself that he might be right. If enough sparks started flying, someone was likely to get burned. And that someone might be her. "I'd better dish up this ice cream before it melts," she said. "Would you like some coffee?"

And so, after all the fireworks between them that night, they sat down peaceably enough to bowls of ice cream and mugs of hot coffee.

Then Ethan said, "I'd like to explain to you about Beryl, if you'll listen."

Three

"Your relationship with Beryl is no concern of mine." But Jess had a few opinions on the subject just the same. Ethan must have guessed as much, because he gave her a knowing smile.

"I think it is your concern. You obviously disapprove of my eagerness to leap into a new love affair so soon after Beryl's departure. Somehow I've got to convince you I'm not the fickle sort of man you think I am."

"Aren't you?" Jess gave him a skeptical stare over the rim of her coffee mug.

"No. I'll admit that tonight everything happened so fast that it might seem that way. But *you* are mostly to blame." His eyes connected with hers in a head-on clash, and then he said softly, "Falling in love at the drop of a hat was never my style . . . before I met you."

"What about falling *out* of love? You seem to have done that rather quickly without my help," Jess pointed out, choosing to ignore the other absurd implications of his remark.

"Beryl and I were never in love. But it's true that our relationship ended abruptly. How could it continue, after the things she said to me tonight? It was over even before she walked out and you walked in."

"Just because of that silly quarrel?" Jess asked, somewhat indignantly, and when Ethan nodded in tight-lipped silence, she charged immediately into impassioned speech. "I'm afraid I can't have much respect for a man who would end a relationship over something so trivial! I'll admit that Beryl had quite a tantrum tonight, but she had some provocation, after all! Most people would be upset by cold showers and wet hair and blown fuses after a long drive, and on an empty stomach. Especially if they were expecting a more romantic getaway than this."

"Don't you mean more *expensive*? You're missing the point."

"Just let me finish. The point is, if you really cared about Beryl, you'd be a lot more understanding and forgiving. But no, the minute she loses her temper and shows some human imperfections, you drop her like a hot potato!"

"Tell me, don't you think she meant it when she accused me of *insulting* her by not spending more money on her? Or didn't you hear that part?" His voice was very quiet, but there was no escaping the powerful intensity of his tawny gaze.

"I heard," Jess answered reluctantly.

"Then, don't you see? When Beryl said *that*, I suddenly realized what I should have seen before— that her values and mine are miles apart. I don't measure my feelings in dollars and cents, but it seems she does. And I want to know that my friends care about *me*, not my bank account."

Jess was suddenly confused. Didn't Ethan realize how much his *own* opinions were influenced by financial considerations? In the business world, "good" was measured and defined in monetary terms, and profit was the ultimate motivation. Ethan operated successfully in that world, so how could he claim that his values were so much purer than Beryl's?

"Do you think it's fair for you to sit in judgment?" Jess asked.

"I didn't think I *was*. I'm just saying that Beryl and I are too different to be happy together. A case of basic, fundamental incompatibility. We'd always be disappointing each other, the way I disappointed her by bringing her here. I love this place—it's like a part of myself—and I wouldn't share it with someone I didn't care for. But she thought I was either too cheap or too ashamed of her to take her to some jet-setters' plastic paradise!"

"I see. So you did care about her?"

"Of course."

"Then how can you end it, just like that, without a backward glance? How can your feelings for her simply vanish?"

"You missed your calling—you should have been a lawyer! And why are you cross-examining me about something you claim isn't even your concern?"

"Are you refusing to answer?" Jess countered quickly, not wanting to examine too closely why she was so interested.

"No. I'll answer. My feelings for Beryl haven't vanished—they've simply changed. I feel the sort of friendly concern for her that I might feel for anyone. We were still in the process of getting to know each other. We hadn't made any kind of commitment. If I'd been deeply in love with her, that would be another story. As it is, the relationship didn't have any future, so there was no point in continuing it."

"Wouldn't it have been better to find that out before you started sleeping together?"

"Now who's sitting in judgment? Human relationships don't always happen logically. You don't learn everything about a person all at once, as if it were data ready to be fed into a computer and analyzed. People make mistakes." He sighed and then shot her a challenging look. "What about you? Haven't you ever gotten involved with a man who later turned out to be all wrong for you?"

"As a matter of fact, I have," Jess confessed, thinking of her brief engagement to Cliff. That was one mistake she'd never make again.

"Then, you know how it happens. The qualities that draw two people together aren't necessarily the ones that will keep them together. Quite the reverse, sometimes. For instance, I was attracted to Beryl partly because she brought out the protective instinct in me." He met Jess's look of surprised disbelief. "Oh, yes. I sensed a lot of insecurity and self-doubt under her pose of aloof sophistication, and I wanted to be the one to help her, reassure her, build up her self-confidence. But ironically enough, it was probably that same self-doubt that led her to put so much faith in money and material possessions. Unlike you, she didn't believe in herself and her own opinions, so the only way she knew how to judge a thing's worth was by its price tag. And so she thought I didn't value *her*, because I tried to offer her something money couldn't buy."

For once, Jess had no reply. She was surprised by Ethan's perceptiveness, and she could no longer presume to criticize the end of his affair with Beryl. Hadn't the mismatch between herself and Cliff happened in much the same way? Cliff had been attracted to her because he'd assumed an artist would be somehow more glamorous, passionate, and exotic than other women. But once attracted, he'd resented her artistic career and tried to turn Jess into a photocopy of the wives and girlfriends of his acquaintances. For her part, Jess had been drawn to Cliff by his arrogant, take-charge personality, his sexuality, his aura of success—the same qualities she had come to hate and fear once he began using them against her, trying to undermine her dedication to her work and her faith in herself.

"So now do you understand about Beryl?" Ethan challenged her, and Jess nodded. "Good. Then we can start talking about *us* again."

Jess felt her pulse leap. "No!" she said quickly.

"Why not? Haven't I just explained away all the obstacles between us?"

Jess had to laugh at his overconfidence, but her laughter ended in an exasperated sigh. She would have to set him straight once and for all.

"Ethan," she said gently. "You've just finished pointing out that people are often attracted to each other for all the wrong reasons, and I know from experience that it's true. In fact, it's probably true in this case! So how can you expect me to get involved with you on the strength of only a few hours' acquaintance? Even if this sudden infatuation of yours is sincere—"

"Dammit!" he cut her off. "It's not fake and it's not infatuation! I've been looking for you long enough to know you when I find you!"

Jess wouldn't let him see how his declaration had shaken her. He sounded so *sure*. "Maybe you thought that about Beryl too . . . once."

"I never thought that about Beryl. There's no comparison! My relationship with her began with my urge to help her. *This* relationship is starting with a hell of a lot more. I admire your work, your humor, and your strength and belief in your self. We have a lot in common, Jess. You and I were meant to be friends."

"Friends?"

"And lovers too." His voice was deep as velvet, and Jess felt breathless and dizzy. His words touched off a sensation akin to a molten lava flow at the very core of her. "You'll never convince me you don't feel it too—this incredible physical attraction between us. Right now all I want is to take you in my arms and make love to you until you cry out because it's so good you can't bear it. Because I know that's how good it'll be for me too."

"Stop it!" She gasped, struggling for inner control. She wouldn't let him seduce her with words.

"I'm just telling you what I want. Don't you want it too?"

"No! We've been through this already, Ethan. I'm not going to hop into bed with you. I'm not even convinced we could be friends, much less lovers."

"You've got it backward. Of course we could be

lovers. Any man and woman could be lovers, just by virtue of a simple physical act. But not every man and every woman could be friends. That requires so much more. And I think we've got what it takes."

"I don't understand you!" Jess exclaimed in confusion. "One minute you say one thing, and the next minute you seem to say the opposite. What do you want from me?"

"Everything. But most of all, I want you to give our friendship a chance."

"We don't even *have* a friendship. And we never will if you keep pressuring me sexually!" Jess's silvery-green eyes were half-pleading, half-angry.

"Very well, then. No more pressure. Much as it goes against my inclinations, I agree to leave sex out of this until you're sure we're ready for it."

Jess gave him a wary look of disbelief. "That could be never," she warned.

"I'm prepared to wait," he said, giving her one of his unblinking, catlike stares. "Just so long as you're willing to try to be friends."

"Friends it is," Jess agreed reluctantly, wondering just how big a fool she was to give this predatory male any kind of foothold in her life. He was still stalking her, even though he'd agreed to change his tactics. But he hadn't left her much choice. If she didn't go along with his "friendship" pact, he might try sweeping her off her feet with his animal magnetism. And Jess wasn't exactly brimming with confidence about her ability to resist him.

Besides, friendship with a man like Ethan might not be half bad. They could probably have a lot of fun together, so long as she was careful never to let it go beyond friendship. She mustn't forget that they were basically incompatible, just as he and Beryl, and she and Cliff, had been. A deeper involvement between them would only lead to trouble. And heartache.

"You don't seem too sure about it," Ethan said, a quizzical expression on his face.

"But I *am*," Jess said, with more firmness than

was warranted by her inner state of doubt. "I'll even shake hands on it." And she held out one slim hand, regretting the gesture as soon as she felt the seductive clasp of Ethan's large hand on hers.

"I'd rather seal it with a kiss," he murmured wickedly, and Jess was immediately indignant.

"No. No kisses. Don't you even talk to me about kisses, unless you want to kiss the whole thing good-bye!"

"Definitely not." He smiled warmly, caressingly, and Jess's heart went through a whole gymnastic routine of somersaults and backflips, until she realized that her hand was still in his possession. She tugged at it, and he released her. "I'll see you tomorrow," he promised. "Thanks for . . . everything."

"Good night." But just as he opened the door, he turned back.

"If I play my clarinet awhile, do you think the noise will bother you?"

"I'll pound on the wall if it does," Jess managed to answer, hiding her surprise at learning of yet another facet to the personality of this hardheaded businessman.

Before long, the night was filled with lilting, mellow clarinet music that crept in like ocean fog. It was moody, temperamental music that gave Jess a very restless feeling. She took out her sketchbook and found herself trying to capture on paper a certain elusive male profile and a heart-tugging smile.

The sky was still overcast the next morning when Jess left the cabin. The sea air was damp, tangy. She walked to a spot where stunted cypress trees screened her from the cabins and went through a brief series of warm-up exercises. Then she began her morning run along the trail that skirted the rim of the headlands. On one side was the drop to the cold, restless green sea, and on the other were open spaces of grass and low-growing brambles, running inland toward the steep, wooded coastal hills. A sea gull cried and swooped in the sky above, and Jess felt a joy as if she herself were part of that wind-borne flight.

She passed the familiar landmarks. Here was the steep descent to the little cove, with its postage stamp of driftwood-strewn beach, where she sometimes went to paint or sunbathe. Farther along was a scattering of very fancy beach houses, part of an exclusive new housing development that looked down its collective nose at Bill's Cabins, the shabby old-timer in the neighborhood. When the trail turned inland to run alongside an old split-rail fence, it was time for Jess to turn back.

She as almost halfway back to the cabins when the figure of another runner appeared in the distance, moving toward her along the trail. Even from this far away it was unmistakably Ethan, and Jess immediately felt self-conscious. Her baggy gray warm-up suit was unflattering, her flyaway hair was tangled, and she was sweaty and out of breath. She didn't know that her green eyes sparkled and her face glowed with health and exuberance.

When the two runners were almost abreast of each other, Ethan motioned Jess to stop. He greeted her with a warm smile. "I see we have something else in common besides our fondness for good food."

"I don't know about you, but it's my fondness for food that got me started running. I was afraid of turning into a blimp."

"Not much chance of *that*," he drawled, giving her a quick up-and-down look that made Jess hope she didn't look as much of a mess as she felt. She noticed resentfully that Ethan looked as fresh as the proverbial daisy. The only sign of his recent exercise was the strong pumping of his chest beneath his form-fitting navy blue jogging suit. His body seemed charged with vitality, as if his touch might transmit a powerful current. "Speaking of my fondness for food," he went on, "I was wondering if . . ."

Jess took one look at the unusually humble and

apologetic look on his face and had to laugh. "Are you asking me for some breakfast?"

"Not only are you beautiful and intelligent, but you're a mind reader! If you could just lend me some eggs and a slice of bread and a cup of coffee—"

"Don't be silly. This is the perfect excuse for making pancakes, and I'd be a fool to pass it up! Just give me a chance to get dressed, and then come on over to my place."

"Bless you! I promise I'll do the dishes this time."

Jess fairly flew back to the cabin while Ethan continued his morning run. She refused to listen to the inner voice that asked her why she was so pleased at the idea of making his breakfast.

She kept her shower brief, knowing that Ethan would need hot water very shortly. Dressed in her usual jeans, T-shirt, and sweater, with her hair freshly combed and braided, Jess tidied the minuscule kitchen area and set about mixing up some pancake batter. It seemed no time at all before Ethan was there, his hair still wet from the shower. He cracked jokes and demolished every pancake Jess set before him. When the sun broke through the clouds and shone cheerfully while they finished their mugs of coffee, Jess found herself feeling perilously happy. Much too happy. Friendship was all very well, but it wasn't wise to go on sharing meals with this man.

With this in mind, she made some sandwiches for Ethan's lunch and then offered to drive him into Mendocino to buy groceries. "We can go after three," she said. "I'll quit painting a couple of hours early today. That is, if you trust yourself in my car."

"I'll take my chances. Should I fear the driver or the vehicle itself?"

"Wait and see!"

Six hours later Jess found herself grinning as she watched Ethan gingerly fold his six-foot-plus frame into the passenger seat of her much-abused old VW bug. The little car was almost twenty years old and needed a new paint job and just about everything else, but Jess felt a certain affection for "Old Betsy," as she had nicknamed the temperamental auto. Old Betsy had probably gone through several owners by the time Jess bought her for a song just after graduating from college.

"Will she make it all the way into town?" Ethan asked.

"Oh, ye of little faith! She made it all the way up here from San Francisco, didn't she? And that trip's no picnic."

It wasn't a long drive from Bill's Cabins to Mendocino. Jess quickly traversed the network of back roads that brought them to the main highway, which on this brief but much-traveled stretch between Mendocino and Fort Bragg had been widened to four lanes. Highway 1 wasn't as picturesque here as it was when it snaked right along the coastal cliffs, hugging all the curves of the continent's western edge, but it was certainly less nerve-racking to drive.

Jess was in high spirits. Her painting had gone well and it was a beautiful afternoon. The sun was absurdly warm for late October, and it glinted on yellow foliage that stood out against the surrounding dark pines. She took the turnoff onto the Mendocino headland, passing several large Victorian houses that had been converted to bed-and-breakfast inns. Turning onto the main street, she could look off to her left and see distant waves dancing in the sunlight across the bay.

"You picked a good season for your holiday," Ethan remarked. "During the summer this town is wall-to-wall tourists and perpetual fog. But you should come again sometime in the spring, when the grass is emerald green and the whole headland is carpeted with wild flowers."

"It sounds heavenly." Jess had been entranced since her first glimpse of the town a week ago, when she saw its gingerbread-trimmed houses, weathered wooden water towers, and white-steepled church facing her as she drove north across the mouth of the Big River. More intimate acquaintance had not changed her first, favorable impression. The town had sprung up in the mid-nineteenth century around its lumber mill, but the mill had been gone for decades now, along with the original redwood forests. These days, Mendocino was a thriving artists' colony, and it was that reputation that had prompted Jess to spend her vacation here.

After parking the car, Jess agreed to meet Ethan for coffee in an hour, once he'd done his shopping. She loved wandering around Mendocino, browsing in the many art galleries and craft shops and delighting in the bright little flower gardens tucked away in odd corners. The houses fascinated her too. Cheek by jowl with the mansions of long-dead lumber barons stood tumbledown shacks that nowadays probably carried hefty price tags, since the village had been caught up in the tourist boom. And whenever Jess tired of such sights, there was always the ever-changing spectacle of the sea, only a five-minute walk away, across the open expanse of the state-preserved headland.

Jess was in a contented mood after her pleasant ramble, but her peace was shattered by Ethan's first words to her once they had ordered croissants and cappuccino in the cozy little coffee shop.

"I have a proposition to make," he said. "I've just been calling about my car. Thank goodness Beryl managed to get it back to my place in one piece, but it seems there's nobody free to drive it back up here for several days. Would it be possible for you and Old Betsy to haul me around until then? Of course I'll pay for the gas, meals, and all that."

"But couldn't you just rent a car?" Jess asked in dismay, and then realized how ungracious she sounded. "I mean, this is a *working* holiday for me. I don't have time to play chauffeur. I'm sorry." But her biggest objection was one she kept to herself— she was afraid of the long-term effects of Ethan's undeniable sex appeal if she spent too much time with him.

"I promise you'll have plenty of time for painting,

and it would do you good to get out and do some sight-seeing. Have you seen any of the coast besides this stretch between Mendocino and Fort Bragg?"

"Not really, but—"

"If you went to Rome or Paris, would you lock yourself in your room and simply paint what was already in your head, without even trying to see and experience new things?"

"Of course not, but—"

"But that's exactly what you're doing here."

She had to laugh. "That's not true! Everywhere I turn I see enough to keep me painting for months! What could you show me that would be so much better?"

"Plenty! Jess, I know this coast like the back of my hand. I come here every year and go around to all the special places I first discovered as a boy. I could share those places with you, and tell you what I know about the coast and its moods and its history. You do want a deeper understanding than you'd get from a picture postcard, don't you?"

"Of course, but—"

"Don't you know any words besides 'but'? You wouldn't have to do that much driving, you know. Once we reached a particular spot, you could set up your easel and paint for hours while I rambled around. I respect your need to work but I honestly don't think this would interfere. Trust me. You could always call a halt if it didn't work out."

Jess felt herself weakening. It was true that so far she'd only seen the coast through a tourist's eyes, and she could well imagine what depths of mood and feeling might be added to her paintings if she went along with Ethan's proposal. And she'd probably have fun. So the question now was—did she think she could handle that many hours of proximity to Ethan Jamieson? And was she going to let herself be scared away from a learning experience that might prove beneficial to her work? Put like that, the answer was obvious.

"I'll do it. You've got yourself a car and a driver,

such as they are," she announced. "When do we start?"

"How about tonight? We can celebrate our new partnership over dinner at a cozy little restaurant I know."

"But Ethan—" Another intimate dinner à *deux* had not been what Jess had in mind when she agreed to his plan.

"No more buts, Jess. You wouldn't abandon me to eating there by myself, would you?"

But she might have done exactly that if she could have foreseen where it all would lead.

Four

The evening got off to a bad start. By the time Jess knocked at Ethan's door to let him know she was ready to leave for the restaurant, she'd had plenty of time to realize what a big mistake she was making. She'd go with him tonight, but this was positively the last meal they would share together. The less she saw of Ethan, the better off she'd be. Little did she know how much *more* of Ethan she was about to see, in the most literal sense.

She knocked and waited, and then knocked again. When Ethan finally opened the door he was naked except for a towel draped casually around his waist. The towel clung damply to the strong, sleek curves of his muscled hips and thighs, and its whiteness contrasted sharply with the tanned, moist flesh that rippled like golden-brown silk above and below the brief white rectangle of cloth.

Jess was stricken by a traitorous urge to touch his glistening bare skin. Water droplets had gathered in the hollows above the hard line of his collarbone, and the hair on his chest was beaded with moisture. Her lips quivered with sudden thirst for the wetness of his flesh, and her mouth tingled at the thought of the taste and feel of him against her tongue.

"My dear lady! If you could only see the expression on your face!" His voice was full of devilish laughter, and so were his eyes. "You make me feel like a giant ice cream cone about to be licked."

"You're flattering yourself again," Jess managed to retort coldly as she brought her wayward imagination under control. "If I look hungry it's because I *am* hungry . . . for my dinner! And I doubt if even you could charm or bribe your way into a restaurant dressed like that, so please hurry up and put some clothes on!"

"My humblest apologies for keeping you waiting. You look sensational in that dress. Would you believe *I* couldn't find a thing to wear?"

"No." Her tone was icy, but Jess was very much afraid that Ethan hadn't missed the way her lips twitched with amusement.

"I didn't think you'd buy that. Would you believe I'm not ready yet because I didn't want to seem overeager on our first date?" His anxious, confiding look was so comically disarming that Jess took refuge in sarcasm.

"I've got news for you, Ethan. Answering the door practically naked on a first date is about as overeager as you can get. Though I'd hardly call this a 'date,'" she hastened to add.

"What about *completely* naked?" he drawled, smiling wickedly as he hooked his thumbs over the top edge of the towel so that it slid perceptibly lower on his hips, revealing a band of untanned skin. "Where would that register on the overeagerness scale?"

He was outrageous! Jess knew he was trying to force her into laughter, but at the same time she couldn't be sure this unpredictable man wouldn't actually drop that towel at any second! Quickly she suppressed the uneasy flicker of excitement that darted through her at the thought. She didn't want him to see that his teasing was having an effect, so she gritted her teeth and gave an impatient sigh.

"No doubt you think you're being dreadfully amusing," she said with all the haughty scorn she could muster. "But I'm too hungry for your brand of humor just now, so will you please shut up and get dressed? I should warn you that I have a tendency to turn very cranky when I don't get my meals on time."

"I'll bear that in mind. God forbid that someone with your sweet, bland, even-tempered disposition should ever get *cranky*!" His eyes danced with gentle mockery, and their golden depths held a warm, almost irresistible invitation to shared laughter. "Would you like to come in and help me get dressed?"

"No! I'll wait next door. And if you aren't ready in ten minutes you can just forget the whole thing. I'll fix my own dinner and you can stay here and eat peanut butter and jelly sandwiches in the nude!" She turned and marched away before he had a chance to come up with any cute remarks on the decadent possibilities of combining nudity with peanut butter.

Five minutes later he showed up at her door, looking casually elegant in a wool blazer and dark slacks. Jess had put those five minutes to good use, strengthening her defenses against his infectious humor and beguiling charm. In fact, her mood had hardened to one of resentment. He'd had no right to try to tantalize her with the sight of all his unclad male pulchritude! Last night he had promised not to pressure her sexually, but already he was cheating on their agreement.

"Something tells me you're mad at me," Ethan said a few minutes later as they walked through the chilly twilight to the car.

"How very observant of you," Jess broke her hostile silence long enough to remark. The full skirt of her camel-colored, lightweight wool dress swished against her legs as she strode briskly along.

"May I ask what I've done, aside from the obvious crime of making us a few minutes late for dinner?" he inquired. Jess stalked grimly on. "For which I do apologize," he added.

When Jess refused to acknowledge his words by even a token shrug of disdain, Ethan thrust himself into her path with such determined suddenness that she walked head-on into the solid wall of his body. She would have fallen backward if his hands hadn't caught her against him. He had planted himself with legs astride to brace himself for their collision, and her hips were now locked against his groin. Jess was instantly aware of the stirring of his flesh where her body pressed so intimately into his.

"Uh-oh—look what you made me do," Ethan said teasingly, but the reckless fire in his eyes warned Jess that the joking might turn all too serious within a second.

"Let go of me!" Jess snapped, horrified at the liquid heat that rippled through her in response to the gently thrusting pressure of his growing arousal.

"Where did your sense of humor vanish to?" he asked, loosening his grip just enough so she could pull back from the enforced intimacy of thigh against thigh.

"There's nothing funny about what you're trying to do, Ethan!" She glared at him with eyes as sharp as shards of tinted green glass. "You aren't keeping your part of the bargain."

"Now, hold on. The bargain was that I wouldn't pressure you into a physical relationship, so we'd have time to get to know each other and become friends. I don't see how a little harmless teasing and flirtation is breaking the rules."

"You call *this* harmless teasing?" Jess demanded indignantly, referring to the way he was holding her.

"As a matter of fact, I do. I agreed to give you breathing space, Jess, but I didn't agree to forget that I'm a man and you're a woman. You turn me on, and it's impossible for me to pretend you don't." He grinned, and let his gaze slip down between their bodies. "Especially at a moment like this."

"You and I obviously have different definitions of the word 'pressure,' " she said.

"True. You seem to think it means anything that might arouse the slightest sexual temptation in you. Allow me to demonstrate my own interpretation. If I were trying to pressure you, do you think I'd make jokes about *this*?" His hands clasped the firm flesh of her buttocks and pulled her roughly against him, so she felt the throbbing male hardness pressing through the light fabric of her skirt. She gasped and tried to break free.

"Do you think I'd let you pull away without trying to kiss you?" he whispered, bringing his lips so close to hers that she felt the warmth and quickness of his breath invade her mouth though his lips never actually touched hers. "Do you think I wouldn't touch you here?" His hand hovered within a hair's breadth of caressing the crest of her breast, and her skin prickled with arousal. "And here?" His hand skimmed down the length of her body, almost but not quite brushing against her, until his fingers spread possessively above the apex of her thighs. The mere suggestion of his touch there triggered a swarm of sensations that left Jess feeling weak and breathless.

"You see," Ethan concluded, stepping suddenly away from her. "*That's* pressure. That's taking advantage of all those physical urges I can arouse in you against your will. But you don't have to be afraid of that, because we have a bargain."

"Like hell I don't have to be afraid!" Jess hissed, furious that she had responded so readily to this devious seduction that pretended to be less than the real thing but was in reality just as effective. "It seems to me you've been trying to take advantage of my 'physical urges' since the moment we met! Our bargain didn't stop you from flaunting yourself at me half-naked tonight. In fact, I think you did it on purpose. You're an unprincipled exhibitionist!"

"How do you figure that?" He sounded amused.

"I didn't hear the shower running when I left my room tonight, so there was no excuse for you to come to the door dressed—or should I say *un*-dressed?—in just a towel. You'd had plenty of time to get ready. The only possible explanation is that you wanted to show off your sexy pectorals."

"My what?" he exclaimed.

"Your damn chest muscles!"

"Thank goodness. When you said 'pectorals' I was afraid I might have sprouted fins without knowing it. But perhaps I could have learned to live with that, just so long as *you* thought they were sexy."

Jess whirled around and stomped off down the path just in time to hide her involuntary grin at the ridiculous thought of Ethan growing fins. The damnable thing was that on him they probably *would* look sexy.

"Don't you want to hear my explanation?" he asked, catching up to her and keeping pace alongside her with ease.

"Not particularly."

"Not even if I confess that your suspicions are one hundred percent correct?"

"What?" She gave him a startled glance.

"I thought that might get your attention," he said with satisfaction. "Yes, Jess, I was deliberately teasing you. I waited until I heard you leave your room and then I turned the shower on just long enough so I'd look authentically wet when I greeted you at the door. Your response was rewarding, to say the least."

She halted in mid-stride. "Why, you . . . you . . . ."

"Temper, temper," Ethan admonished. "Do you realize that you wouldn't be nearly so much fun to provoke if you didn't overreact so spectacularly?"

"I am not overreacting!" Jess exclaimed.

"Of course not," he answered soothingly, as if he were humoring a dangerous lunatic. "Jess, will you please listen to what I'm trying to tell you? We both know that you don't want to be attracted to me. Yet you are. There's no point trying to hide it by getting all huffy and upset. And there's no *need* to hide it, either. I'm not going to pounce on you just because I see that revealing gleam in your eye once in a while.

I intend to keep my side of the bargain. So just relax and be yourself and go with the flow."

Jess gave a deep sigh. She *couldn't* "go with the flow," because it would sweep her straight into his arms. "How can I relax when you insist on turning everything into a sexual confrontation?"

Ethan stared at her in perplexed silence. "Temptation scares you, doesn't it?" he said at last. "I thought you just needed time to get to know me, but I'm beginning to think you don't want to want me *ever*. Am I right?"

Of course he was right, but Jess was reluctant to admit it. She maintained a tight-lipped silence while the gaze of his tiger-striped eyes prowled over her face, stalking the thoughts and emotions she tried to hide.

"It seems to me that *you're* the one who's not keeping our bargain," he accused softly. "You're not giving our friendship a chance."

"What you mean is that I won't give you the chance to talk me into bed!"

"No, what I mean is that your mind is closed tighter than a fist! And that's no way to start a friendship. I get the feeling that when you said, 'Don't pressure me,' what you really meant was, 'Don't try to change my mind.' Can't you see how prejudiced and unfair that is?"

Maybe it was unfair, but that was still the way she felt. She was determined to avoid a sexual entanglement that could only lead to unhappiness. But his accusation had succeeded in making her feel guilty about it.

"Listen to me, Jess," he urged fiercely. "We both know that the final decision about whether the two of us become lovers will rest with you. You're the judge and jury. But I'll be damned if I'll sit back and let you reach a verdict before you've even considered the evidence! So you're just going to have to put up with an occasional reminder that I want our friendship to be more than platonic!" He glared at her as if he expected another defiant rejoinder.

"May we please go eat dinner now?" Jess asked quietly. "You've given me a lot to think about, and I don't think too well on an empty stomach."

Ethan shrugged, and just that brief, controlled flexing of his body was enough to send another thread of sensual awareness weaving through Jess's thoughts. He had the power to awaken her desires without even trying.

The silence between them as they reached the car was like the uneasy, waiting silence between a flash of lightning and the echoing roll of thunder that must follow. Ethan slid into the seat beside Jess with the graceful, sinister ease of a dark snake. She refused to look at him, but the atmosphere of coiled, contained emotion ready to release itself at an instant's notice was too potent to ignore.

They didn't say a word during the drive. Jess concentrated on the road and the oncoming parade of headlights that seemed to intensify the velvety dusk. All the while she was aware of Ethan's dark, watchful presence.

The scene on the path to the parking lot replayed itself in her mind as she drove. She knew she'd handled things badly. If only she hadn't let herself get so upset by his teasing. There was nothing so terribly alarming in his lighthearted sexual skirmishing—not when you compared it to this brooding, smoldering, passion-laden silence that threatened to explode at any second.

Damn the man! She would have to concede his right to a little "harmless flirtation" after all. Now that they'd clarified their bargain, she saw that her expectations had been unrealistic if not unreasonable. She still had no intention of letting Ethan entice her into his bed, but surely there was no need to panic at the first hint of temptation. Let him smile that damn smile of his and whisper suggestive little nothings in her ear and even tantalize her with the sight of his smooth, sculpted flesh—it wasn't going to get him anywhere with her.

Oddly enough, she found herself believing that he

really did intend to keep his part of their bargain. She might disagree with his interpretation of their agreement, but at least it meant that she was safe from the kind of forceful and seductive "pressure" he had demonstrated so effectively tonight. Safe, that is, so long as she had the sense to keep saying no. Safe so long as she didn't let herself be swayed by all that "evidence" he was determined to present.

Jess darted a surreptitious glance at Ethan as they pulled into the restaurant parking lot, and abruptly wondered who she thought she was fooling. *Safe?* With *him?* She must be out of her mind. There was temptation for her in every taut, muscled fiber of this man's body.

He uncoiled himself from his seat with the smoothness of a well-oiled precision instrument. As he stepped quickly to her side, Jess felt a flutter of panic as if her brave thoughts just moments ago had never been.

"Promise you won't bite me if I take your arm?" he asked in a low, gravelly voice that startled a shiver of reaction up her spine.

"I'm not quite *that* hungry yet. Or even that cranky," she reassured him.

"Good. Then, there's hope," he said as he tucked her arm in his and headed across the parking lot.

"Hope for what?" Jess asked breathlessly, wishing her body hadn't reacted to his casual touch with such instant sensual awareness.

"Hope for us to spend a pleasant evening together learning how to be friends." He hesitated a second, tossing her a quick, rueful smile. "We both seem to need a little practice at it."

"That sounds suspiciously like an apology." She returned his smile and held her breath, waiting for his response.

"Then, I guess it is one." He grunted. "As long as you don't expect me to take back what I said. I still intend to convince you that we belong in each other's arms," he warned her. "But maybe I did come on a bit strong tonight."

"And maybe I did overreact, just a little. I suppose it's only fair that I let you 'argue your case' now and then. But from now on, *please* keep your clothes on. And no more of that mmm . . . uh . . . pelvic contact."

"Agreed. How can I refuse you anything when you blush like that? Tell me, does your entire body turn that same wacky shade of pink?"

"I wouldn't know; I've never looked to see," Jess answered crisply as they entered the restaurant. But she wasn't being completely honest. If the waves of heat that crept down over her breasts, belly, and thighs were any indication, that "wacky" shade of pink was covering every inch of her.

The next two hours were delightful. Jess felt herself relaxing under the soothing influence of the delicious food and the wine, and the pleasing elegance of her surroundings. Perhaps all that earlier tension had been caused by hunger, because she certainly didn't feel one bit tense or cranky now.

In fact, she felt so mellow, she found herself positively beaming at Ethan across the snowy tablecloth and the crystal wineglasses and the cut flowers. He was so much fun to talk to when he wasn't probing for her sexual vulnerabilities.

Their quiet laughter rang out with ever-increasing frequency as the evening progressed. Ethan's eyes glowed beguilingly in the candlelight, and Jess never stopped to think what messages her own eyes might be radiating. Happiness seemed to effervesce inside her like champagne bubbles every time Ethan smiled.

"What *did* you hope to gain by flaunting yourself at me wearing next to nothing?" she asked at last in fearless curiosity as they lingered over liqueurs and demitasse cups of strong, rich coffee. "Didn't you realize how angry I'd be?"

"I thought you'd be more amused than angry. And you *were* amused, at first." He gave a slow grin. "You also seemed a mite impressed by my manly charms."

"I've seen better!" Jess retorted saucily though not quite truthfully.

Ethan's low, rich chuckle showed he wasn't the least bit daunted. "I wasn't trying to win any beauty contests. But I did hope my presentation of the 'bare facts' might make a favorable impression on you."

Jess gave an appreciatively disgusted groan at both his pun and his conceit. "You'll need more compelling 'evidence' than that to win your case," she said, and then wished she hadn't made her words sound so much like a dare.

Ethan merely looked amused. "How true. We'll label your reaction to my 'sexy pectorals' as Exhibit A and go on from there."

It seemed to Jess that "go on from there" had a rather ominous ring to it, but in her present relaxed and happy mood she wasn't about to get all irate and panicky. She did wonder, as they left the restaurant, if she was quite clearheaded enough for the drive back to Bill's. She shouldn't have had that third glass of wine, much less the after-dinner sips of Amaretto.

"Would you like me to drive?" Ethan offered quietly, and Jess noticed with some resentment that he looked perfectly sober. Not even one dark, silky lock of hair was out of place, and no tinge of added color mottled his high cheekbones. His eyes were calm and smiling, and his gait was still the same forceful stride it always was. How unfair.

"That might be safer," she conceded sulkily. She tossed the car keys at him, and he fielded her wide throw with graceful expertise. No need to worry that *his* reflexes were under the influence.

As Ethan piloted Old Betsy along the dark highway, Jess leaned her face into the cold, damp rush of air from her open window, hoping it would blow the fuzziness out of her head. All the moist, ferny scents of the night and the pungent, complex odors of the sea seemed to mingle in an intoxicating appeal to her sensual side.

"Let's stop here," she declared abruptly, forgetting

everything but her sudden desire to experience first-hand the sights and sounds and smells of the night. It was so different from nighttime in the city.

"Can you wait till we get across this bridge?" Ethan asked, rather anxiously.

"Of course!" Jess laughed. "What do you think I'm going to do—explode?" Immediately after the bridge, Ethan turned onto a road that led down to the small beach that formed at the river's mouth. Jess bounded out of the car, sniffing the air expectantly. "Well, aren't you going to get out?" she teased Ethan, who hadn't yet budged from behind the wheel.

"Wouldn't you rather . . . have some privacy?" he asked in awkward surprise.

"What for?"

"You mean you aren't going to be sick? When you asked me to stop the car in the middle of the bridge, I thought—"

Jess laughed again. "You thought I was ready to lose my cookies—or rather my peaches flambé! Don't worry. I feel wonderful."

"Where are you going?" he asked, stepping out of the car as Jess started to follow the sound of the waves that ceaselessly nudged the dark shoreline.

"For a walk, silly! Do you want to come too?"

Wordlessly he joined her, and Jess was glad of the support of his arm as she began to make her way across the sand. There was moonlight, but it was obscured and diffused by the low-lying coastal clouds, so Jess couldn't see well enough to avoid every piece of driftwood and clump of decaying seaweed that lay in her path. Being slightly tipsy didn't help matters any.

They crossed under the span of the highway bridge that arched far above their heads, and now Jess could see the full, dark expanse of beach reaching out to where the water was a pale, whispering gleam in the faint light. Off to their left, someone had lit an illicit campfire, and the soft strumming of a guitar was carried on the breeze along with the tang of woodsmoke.

"Let's sit here and listen," Jess whispered, and Ethan found a spot for them on a log that had been worn smooth by days at sea. The wind was bone-chilling, and after a few minutes of sitting stiffly aloof, Jess allowed herself to slide closer to Ethan's warmth. She didn't even object when his arms slowly wrapped themselves around her shoulders.

Watching the flickering shadows and shooting sparks of the distant fire, Jess felt entranced by the music and the sound of the waves and the thudding of Ethan's heartbeat. They all seemed part of the same primitive magic. When Ethan's hands began a long, slow caress from the nape of her neck down to the base of her spine, that too seemed magical.

"I think it's time for Exhibit B," Ethan murmured, and bent his head to feather her cheeks and brow with fleeting, insubstantial kisses that awakened a hunger for more.

"Objection!" Jess protested breathlessly. "You're badgering the witness. And I thought I said *no kisses.*"

"Objection overruled." Before Jess could utter another word of protest, Ethan's mouth flitted down against hers. His lips and tongue were warm and sweet as they softly possessed her mouth in a delicate, pulsing rhythm that was like the cadence of the guitar music rippling through the night. It wasn't a demanding kiss, but that made it all the harder to resist. His tongue thrust gently between her lips again and again, wearing down her resistance as surely as the waves breaking on the shore could wear away the hardest stone.

His kiss seemed to last forever before he moved his hands to span the light, fragile bones of her rib cage, causing Jess to moan in uneasy pleasure. His thumbs rotated sensuously across the hardened tips of her breasts for brief seconds of fearful ecstasy. His kiss turned hungry and hard, and then he jerked himself away from her yielding softness, gripping her shoulders as if to prevent his hands from once more seeking out her breasts.

"I never thought it could be so damn hard to keep a bargain," he whispered harshly. "Your body's quivering with desire, ready for me to make love to you right here on this beach. I can picture you all pearly white against the sand, whimpering love cries in my ears, arching against me all sweet and silken and fiery. Please, Jess," he pleaded hoarsely. "Tell me that's what you want. Tell me I wouldn't be pressuring you if—"

"You know you would!" Jess managed to gasp out, overcoming the urge to give in to her body's aching demand. For a moment there, desire had clogged her rational thought processes and trapped her willpower in a sweet, sticky lethargy as if her blood had turned to honey in her veins. Never in her life had she wanted a man so much. But never had she been so sure that a man could bring her disaster. "I told you not to kiss me," she reminded him shakily.

"So you did," he said very softly. "Guess I should have listened." He stood up and walked a few feet away. "Are you ready to leave?" His tone was clipped and hard, and Jess felt as if all the evening's magic had withered to dust before her very eyes.

"Yes, let's go," she said wearily. Her head was beginning to ache, and she wondered how she could have been so foolish as to insist they stop in the first place. Any imbecile could have predicted what was likely to happen when a slightly intoxicated female snuggled up to a virile male on a moonlit beach. She must have been out of her mind.

The rest of the journey home was swift and silent. When they reached Jess's door, Ethan grunted something that might have been "good night" or might equally have been "go to hell" and then stalked away. Jess gave a shrug and unlocked her door.

Five

Regardless of her intention not to lose any sleep over Ethan, Jess did lie awake pondering that disastrous scene on the beach. This should be a lesson to her not to give an inch where he was concerned. Once you started giving in to a man like Ethan, life became a constant struggle just to call your soul your own.

It was unsettling to remember how easily she'd fallen prey to Cliff's subtle emotional blackmail. He'd even had her feeling defensive and apologetic about her work as an artist, because of his condescending and belittling attitude toward any activity that didn't pay off in cold, hard cash.

Thank goodness she'd come to her senses and ended her engagement with Cliff before he turned her into a doormat. But now she knew her own weaknesses. She couldn't risk getting involved a second time with anyone who seemed even remotely capable of playing those sorts of mind games with her. And Ethan, with his forceful personality, persuasive charm, and magnetic sensuality, had already demonstrated how quickly he could sway her. But no more. Jess vowed that tomorrow would be a very different story.

Unfortunately, tomorrow came before she was quite ready for it. It was scarcely light outside when Jess was awakened by the sound of cheerful whistling coming from next door. She groaned and pulled the pillow over her head, but still she could hear the thwack of a cracking eggshell. And then another. And another. And . . . She counted eight in all. Eight! That gluttonous pig. Meanwhile the whistling went on, and the eggs were soundly beaten, with quite unnecessary vigor, for several minutes. Then she heard the sound of butter sizzling in a pan.

"Good morning, Jess—I can hear your stomach growling!" The hatefully cheery voice floated through the wall with cavalier disregard for truth and decorum. Her stomach had not growled, and she found his implication that he could actually hear her every intimate little sound in very poor taste indeed.

"Wake up, sleepyhead!" he called impatiently. "I'm fixing you one of my infamous green chili omelets with jack cheese."

"Don't bother. I'm not hungry," she snarled, trying unsuccessfully to ignore the enticing odor that now wafted into the room. If she didn't get out of here immediately, her hunger pangs were going to betray her into letting Ethan win yet another moral victory.

Muttering in disgust, Jess leaped out of bed, flung on some clothes, gathered up her painting gear, and slammed out the door. There were several good break-fast places in Mendocino, and somehow she would survive without a cup of coffee until she got there. Somehow.

Jess was almost to the parking lot before she heard the brisk tramping of feet right behind her. "Where are we off to today?" Ethan inquired in a vigorous voice bursting with cheerfulness. His smile looked unquenchable, but that didn't stop Jess from trying.

"*We* are going nowhere," she said blightingly. "I'd like some time to myself, if you don't mind. I've got a lot of work to do and no time for your sort of fun and games."

"No time for breakfast either? And no time to wash the sleep out of your eyes?"

"Will you mind your own business?" She turned on him fiercely as they reached the parking lot.

"But it *is* my business. I've got a responsibility to the unsuspecting public. I can't unleash you on the world before you're wide enough awake to be semi-human! Have some coffee." He had slung his backpack off his shoulder and pulled out a Thermos, and now he presented her with a cup of steaming, aromatic dark liquid. To Jess's quivering nostrils it smelled like the promise of heaven, and she couldn't hold back from reaching out for the cup.

"And a few bites of this omelet," Ethan ordered, drawing a small covered dish out of his pack with all the flourish of a magician pulling rabbits out of a hat. Gently he guided her unresisting body into a sitting position on one of the logs that marked the boundaries of the parking lot. When he lifted the lid off the omelet and placed the dish in her lap, Jess felt her senses swim with hunger at the delectable smell. Like someone in a trance, she gripped the fork Ethan put in her hand, and began to eat. If *this* was being manipulated, it wasn't half bad.

"How about doing some ghost-hunting today?" Ethan coaxed, seizing the moment when her hunger-dazed resistance was at its nadir. "I can show you the remnants of some of the old doghole lumber ports that used to line the coast north of here."

"Dog-*what*?" Jess inquired with her mouth full of the spicy omelet.

"Doghole ports. They were called that because just about every cove and inlet big enough for a dog to turn around in had one." He brought a map out of his capacious pack and began pointing to tiny dots along the shoreline. His arm brushed against Jess, and his head was bent so close to hers that she could easily have leaned over to kiss the nape of his neck. But of course she did no such thing.

"What happened to them?" she asked, trying to

concentrate on the map though her attention was riveted by Ethan's nearness.

"Once the railroad came through to the coast at Fort Bragg, these ports were no longer needed for shipping lumber. And the nearby stands of timber had already been logged out by then. So the towns just died. I thought seeing them might give you a better sense of the history behind all the pretty scenery." His smile dared her to take the challenge.

"You win," Jess said with a sigh as she swallowed the last tasty morsel of the omelet. "We'll go look at ghost towns today. But if I find it's interfering with my work . . ."

"It won't." And he was right. Seldom had Jess experienced a more productive day. Ethan was able to show her not only new sights but also a new way of seeing them. His tales of the harsh lives of the early settlers and the treacherous power of the sea that could batter ships into driftwood on the rocky cliffs gave her a sense of the darker, grimmer side of the beauty she saw around her. It was exciting to see that new vision taking subtle shape in her sketches.

At first Ethan showed a distracting tendency to try to carry on a conversation while she attempted to work, and that reminded her unpleasantly of Cliff. She had always been infuriated by Cliff's assumption that it was okay to interrupt her concentration with a constant flow of small talk. It had been one more way of showing that he considered her work to be of no importance whatsoever. And he'd had a habit of turning up unexpectedly to demand her attention just when she'd told him she would need time alone to work.

But at least Ethan seemed perfectly ready to extend her the courtesy of his silence when she explained that she had difficulty talking and sketching at the same time. She was surprised by how contented he seemed to be with just his own thoughts and the breathtaking scenery for company. Not like most people nowadays, who felt uneasy without something to keep them busy or distracted.

"Don't you get bored just hanging around while I'm working?" Jess asked curiously as they ate the lunch Ethan had packed in his trusty backpack.

"No, I've got great inner resources," he boasted dryly. "Or you could say I'm just lazy," he added with a grin. "I love having the time to lie here looking at the sky, just thinking and dreaming and planning and wondering."

Jess took him at his word, and worked on until the lengthening shadows indicated it was getting late. She was exhausted, and the thought of fixing a meal tonight had no appeal at all. So it was hardly surprising that she agreed to Ethan's suggestion that they stop at a little place he knew that served wonderful Mexican food.

"There goes my diet," she sighed later as she cleaned her plate.

"You don't need to diet," Ethan insisted with a lascivious wink. "But if you're so worried about it, why don't we go jogging together tomorrow morning?"

So she ended up agreeing to that too. And then it seemed silly not to agree to spend the day with him, especially when today had worked out so well. As a tour guide, he was excellent. As a dinner companion, he was delightful. And as long as he didn't try to demonstrate how truly sensational he must be as a lover, what valid reason did she have for avoiding him?

Three days later Jess was still trying to answer that question as they drove inland in search of sunshine on a morning when the coast was inundated by fog.

"What *do* you do for a living?" she asked suddenly of the man sitting next to her. "I just realized, you could be a hit man for the Mafia, for all I know. All that stuff you told me the night we met sounds like a bunch of gobbledygook that could mean anything."

"So you're finally getting curious about me," he said with satisfaction. "That's a good sign."

"Sign of what?" she asked suspiciously.

"That our friendship is getting somewhere at last. Soon we'll be sharing our life stories and telling each other intimate secrets." Something about the way he said "intimate secrets," in that deep, rich voice of his, was suggestively evocative of sexual images. Quickly Jess had to banish the mental picture of Ethan's naked body entwined with hers and his husky voice murmuring soft words in her ears.

"Is asking about your job such a personal question?" she demanded impatiently.

"Not at all." He tossed her a quick smile. "I'm a partner in a chain of gourmet and specialty food stores in the Bay Area, and my area of expertise is predicting food trends and coming up with periodic innovations and creative marketing ideas. It's my job to make sure Fiori's is the first in town to offer croissants at their deli counter and *gelato* in their ice cream freezer, for instance."

"Did you say Fiori's?" Jess's jaw dropped in amazement. "That's my favorite store in the whole world! Of course I can't afford to buy my weekly groceries there, but it's where I always go when I want to splurge on something special like fresh seafood or imported chocolate or a good bottle of wine." She was genuinely impressed. "No wonder you know so much about food."

"You sound positively reverent," Ethan said with a chuckle. "I should have guessed that the quickest way to your heart would be to reveal my association with Fiori's. All this time I could have been wooing you with promises of free slices of linzer torte."

"I'm not quite that easy. Throw in a lifetime supply of Alaskan king crab legs and I might be tempted."

"You've got yourself a deal! Pull the car over right this minute so I can start ravishing you, woman!"

Jess felt she'd better do as he suggested, but only because he was making her laugh, and that interfered with her driving. Sometime during the past few days she'd given up trying to hold back her involuntary response to Ethan's outrageous sense of humor.

"No, stop that!" she protested as Ethan clasped her in his arms and tried to plant a lusty kiss upon her lips. "I only said I *might* be tempted!" Breathless with laughter, she struggled to fend off his marauding mouth.

"Tease!" he accused her, grinning as he trapped her hands in his and held her at his mercy. And then the grin faltered on his face as they both became aware of the sexual tension that suddenly vibrated between them like desert heat in the confined space of the little car.

His eyes assessed her with a keen, calculating light, and Jess sensed the fettered energy of his muscled body. For three days he had scarcely touched her, lulling her into a false sense of security, but it had all been an elaborate game of cat and mouse. And she was the mouse.

She stiffened in apprehension and—dare she confess it, even to herself?—anticipation. Her breath came hard and fast, and her skin was crawling with a sensation she would have liked to think was repulsion, but it was too pleasurably exciting to be that.

Ethan's breath fanned her face as slowly, slowly he bent his head. Every muscle in her body clenched as his tautly sensual mouth inched closer. When he skimmed the corner of her mouth with merely a light, brushing caress of his lips, the implosion of sensation throughout her tense, expectant body had the magnitude of a minor earthquake.

He drew away, breathing unevenly, and a bead of perspiration slid down the side of his face. Desire was like a miasma in the air between them, thick as the fog that cloaked the trees outside the car windows. Raw and potent, it seemed to catch at Jess's throat as she tried to speak.

"I said no kisses," she whispered at last, through

lips that ached and trembled with longing for the full, crushing impact of his mouth's possession.

"I remember," he said softly, and his voice rumbled with a hint of bitter laughter. "Which is why I didn't give you a real kiss after all. That little peck on the edge of your lips hardly counts, now, does it?"

"I guess not," Jess answered quietly, turning the key in the ignition to start the car again. But she knew that for her, that almost-kiss had definitely "counted." She could feel the tendrils of awakened desire unfurling inside her like new green leaves of spring.

"What have you got against me, anyway?" Ethan asked suddenly, startling her.

"Nothing, of course." She tried to sound astonished that he could even ask such a thing, and meanwhile she gripped the steering wheel just a bit harder than usual.

"Then, why won't you let me get close to you, Jess? And I don't mean just sexually! Every time I try to talk to you about *feelings*, either yours or mine, you end up changing the subject or making a joke."

"You're a fine one to complain about *me* making jokes!"

"And now you're doing it again," he accused. "The issue here is not who makes the most jokes! What I'm talking about is the way you wriggle out of every attempt I make at an honest-to-goodness personal conversation."

"Do I really do that?" Jess asked, and this time her surprise was genuine. "I had no idea." But now that she thought about it, it made perfect sense. Unconsciously she had been protecting herself against greater emotional intimacy with Ethan. "What sort of personal conversation did you have in mind?"

"I want to know everything about you, Jess. Where you were born and what your childhood was like. Whether you ever had your tonsils out. How you got started painting. Where you learned to cook. Who your best friend was when you were thirteen. How you feel about your parents. What brand of toothpaste you use. All that important stuff."

"But why, Ethan? What's the point?" Jess asked in dismay. She was oddly terrified at the thought of revealing herself to him like that.

"The point is that we're supposed to be friends." His tone was neither judgmental nor reproachful, but Jess felt a heavy weight of guilt settle over her shoulder blades. If she couldn't give him the kind of friendship he was looking for, at least he deserved her honesty.

"I think it's better if our friendship remains a fairly casual one," she replied carefully. "After all, it's not as though we have a lot in common. You're a supermarket magnate and I'm a poverty-stricken artist." She gave an uneasy laugh. "Surely that tells you something about our chances of becoming bosom buddies."

"That doesn't tell me a damn thing!" Ethan spat out with an anger so intense that Jess trembled. "Our occupations and incomes don't define us! And how can you say we have nothing in common, when you won't even give us a chance to find out? If we're so incompatible, how come we've been so happy spending time together here in Mendocino?"

For the second time that morning, Jess pulled off the road. She knew she couldn't drive safely and participate in a shouting match at the same time. Her palms were perspiring and her jaw was tight with tension as she turned to face Ethan.

"First of all, being an artist is about the most important thing in the world to me, so I think my occupation *does* 'define' me. Secondly, the fact that we've enjoyed each other's company for a few days on vacation doesn't make us kindred spirits. Thirdly—" She stopped abruptly. There was no "thirdly," unless she wanted to explain that she was scared to death at the thought of letting him get any closer.

"All that may well be true," Ethan conceded grimly. "But it's still no excuse for refusing even to try to get to know each other on a deeper level. You've made up your mind ahead of time what the outcome will be. And that's wrong."

It was the same argument they'd had before, only this time they weren't talking about sex. Or were they? Every step that brought them closer emotionally made Jess that much more vulnerable to the magnetic pull of the physical attraction between them. If only Ethan weren't so darn *likable.* He represented a threat that could tear her life apart, and yet it was impossible to resist his zany blend of humor, thoughtfulness, and devastating sex appeal.

"You and I aren't all that different, Jess. You may think my work is poles apart from yours, but we have more in common than you realize. My latest project at Fiori's has quite a lot to do with your line of work, as a matter of fact."

"How's that?" Jess was highly skeptical.

"It's my new idea for marketing wine. Up until now, Fiori's has tended to let our well-earned reputation sell our wine for us. After all, we do offer one of the finest and most extensive selections of wine in this country. But now I'm hoping to increase our sales with a new approach. We're redesigning a section of one of our stores to serve as a combination wine shop and art gallery, to be called the Wine Gallery."

His face glowed with proud enthusiasm, and Jess felt her heart sink down through Old Betsy's floorboards. Every word he spoke just increased her sense of how different their values were. No doubt his concept was a clever one, but she was personally offended by the whole idea of using art as part of some slick sales gimmick. And she could just imagine the kind of mediocre "art" that would wind up on the walls of a supermarket, even if it was a "gourmet" supermarket!

"It sounds . . . very interesting," she said in a constricted voice, trying to hide her distaste in order to avoid hurting his feelings.

"You sound as if you hate the idea," Ethan said stonily. "Do you mind telling me why?"

So much for her attempt at hiding her true feelings! "I don't like to see art being commercialized." She could have said more, but that brief statement was enough to rekindle Ethan's anger.

"Dammit, Jess, what kind of holier-than-thou, head-in-the-sand attitude is that? No wonder you aren't making any money as an artist! I think you've got the wrong idea about this gallery. It's—"

"There's no point in discussing it, Ethan! We're never going to agree." With brisk, decisive movements, Jess started the car and pulled back onto the road. That remark of his about her not making any money had just confirmed all her fears about his attitude. And it hurt.

Ethan looked as if he were about to explode into argument, but then his mouth clamped shut and he folded his arms across his chest. He frowned, then issued a single scathing comment: "Lady, when you lock up your mind, you really throw away the key."

After that, his silence was so intense that Jess could have sworn the very air molecules around him were electrically charged.

His mood didn't seem to have improved by the time they left the fog behind and began to wind through sun-gilded valleys where only the last few traces of morning mist remained.

"Turn here," he instructed her, and after a series of turns onto progressively more primitive roads, they pulled up before a yellow farmhouse with a faded red barn out back. An orchard of gnarled apple trees spread out in rows on every side. "Wait here," he ordered.

Ethan vanished around the side of the house, and when he returned several minutes later, he was carrying an empty bushel basket. "You paint and I'll pick," he said tersely before striding off down one of the many green avenues between the low-growing apple trees. With a small sigh, Jess gathered her painting equipment and set out in the opposite direction in search of a likely spot to set up her easel.

Two hours later, the peaceful solitude of the place had eased the tension generated by her confrontation with Ethan. From her vantage point atop a gentle slope behind the barn, Jess surveyed a scene of pastoral tranquility, and her paintbrush was quick and sure as she painted that drowsy autumn landscape. The sun was warm on her bare arms, and the distant humming of bees and the drifting scent of ripened apples helped weave a tapestry of contentment.

"You look flushed and rosy as an apple yourself." Ethan's resonant, caressing tone was as much a surprise as his sudden reappearance at her side. Jess felt her breath catch in her throat as she gazed up into the overpowering warmth of his smile.

"Don't you know it's risky to sneak up on an artist at work?" she scolded. "I might have spoiled my painting when you startled me like that!"

"Never fear. I waited on purpose till you were holding the brush nowhere near the painting."

"Oh." She was mesmerized by the lithe, bronzed vitality of him as he crouched beside the campstool where she sat. The bunching of his thigh muscles beneath the worn denim of his jeans sent a sizzle of sensation along her spine. "Why do you always have to be so damn thoughtful?" she asked in a muffled voice. "And can't you hold a grudge longer than a couple of hours?"

"Nope. Those were always two of my biggest faults," he replied cheerfully. "Were you hoping to continue our quarrel?"

"No. It's just—"

"—that you feel more comfortable with me as something of an enemy than as a friend?"

"Maybe," she admitted, looking away.

"And I thought we were making progress," he said ruefully. "Oh, well, back to the drawing board. How about some lunch? I've got a jug of ice-cold cider that was pressed right here on this very farm."

Jess had no argument with that idea, and soon they were seated on the grass, devouring the sandwiches they'd packed that morning. "What did you do with all those apples you were going to pick?" she asked as Ethan got up to pluck one from a nearby tree. With the edge of his shirt, he polished it to jewellike brightness and then slowly, appreciatively, sank his teeth into the firm, juicy flesh. There was something so unabashedly sensual in the act that Jess couldn't tear her eyes away. "Don't tell me you ate them all."

"If I had, you'd have to carry me home on a stretcher! No, I left a basket of them down by the car. I figure we'll be having apple pie tonight."

"I didn't know pie-making was one of your talents!" Jess teased, feeling quite sure that *she* was the one who'd be stuck with the job. Not that she minded. Homemade apple pie sounded like a great idea.

"I was hoping you could give me a few pointers," Ethan confessed. "The last pie I made was of the mud variety, and even that was about thirty years ago."

"I'll see what I can do," she promised, and was rewarded when he presented her with a carefully burnished apple as he sat down beside her in the long grass. She reached out to accept the offering, but no sooner had Ethan placed the fruit in her palm than he took possession of her wrist. His strong, tanned fingers slid easily up her forearm and over the sensitive skin of her inner elbow, to rest on the smooth, rounded flesh of her upper arm.

His hand cupped the firm, subtle curve of her biceps, and he bent his head to brush his lips along her honey-colored skin. "You're like a golden apple," he murmured. "A golden apple of the sun."

"Isn't that a line from a poem?" Jess asked nervously, trying to ignore the quiver of delight that started up in her at the light touch of his lips along her arm.

" 'The Song of Wandering Aengus,' by William Butler Yeats. One of my favorites," Ethan informed her, and then his tongue flicked lightly against her arm, which he held as if it were a plump, tender ear of corn that he was about to bite into. "It tells about one man's lifelong pursuit of a romantic vision."

Very softly, in a voice as rich and sweet as the afternoon, he recited the poem, and Jess thought she had never heard anything more beautiful. There was music and magic in every line, and she closed her eyes while the words flowed through her.

When the poem ended with the lines about the silver apples of the moon and the golden apples of the sun, Ethan's teeth closed gently over the flesh of her bare arm. His mouth was like wet silk and moist velvet edged with steel, pressing sharp and sweet against her skin. The combination was sensuously devastating, and Jess tried in vain to hold back a moan of voluptuous pleasure.

As if that were his cue, Ethan let his mouth roam higher, skimming back and forth over the glossy smoothness of her tanned shoulders and then nestling in the curve of her neck. His lips plucked forth vibrations of desire from deep within her, and Jess slowly sank back against the cool grass. Soon she would make the effort to call a halt to this madness, she told herself, but not just yet. No, not yet.

While Ethan's lips and tongue were still weaving a spell of hypnotic kisses across Jess's neck and shoulders, his hands met at her waist and began to ease the fabric of her sleeveless top up over her stomach and then over her breasts.

"No," she said weakly, but Ethan's fingers unhooked the front catch of her bra. The pale, milk-white flesh of her breasts spilled into his palms, and he pressed his face against her softness.

"The silver apples of the moon," he whispered huskily, and opened his mouth to taste first one ripe firm orb and then its twin. Pierced by a flash of intense pleasure, Jess almost cried out. A great shimmering pool of desire began a rhythmic ebb and flow within her, and her arms closed convulsively around Ethan's neck, savoring the silken touch of his midnight-dark hair against her bare skin.

Slowly his mouth relinquished possession of her breast and he lifted himself on his arms until he was looking directly into her eyes. "Jess?" he whispered. "I'm probably going to hate myself for asking this, but I need to know. Are you ready for us to be lovers now?"

The pain in her chest was so sudden and intense that she couldn't breathe. Yes, she was physically ready. Hurtfully, shamefully ready, and if he hadn't kept his side of their bargain and given her this final, reasoning moment in which to choose acquiescence or denial, the choice would have been made for her. But he was an honorable man, and so he'd left the final decision up to her, just as he'd promised. Unfortunately, cold, hard reality hadn't been changed during those moments she'd spent floating on Cloud Nine in his embrace, so her answer had to be the same as ever.

He watched the changing expressions flitting like cloud shadows across her face, and he sighed. "Don't tell me—let me test my psychic powers. Your brain still doesn't like me, no matter what the rest of you says, right?"

"It's not that I don't like you," she said quickly. "But my brain is not ready for us to be lovers. I'm sorry I got so carried away that I gave you the wrong signals."

"That's funny—I'm not one bit sorry you got carried away. I'm just sorry you bolted back down to earth so fast. Here, eat your apple," he said, picking up the piece of fruit that had fallen out of Jess's hand during their prolonged embrace. He gazed at it pensively, rubbing his fingertips over its glossy skin, and then began to toss it up and down. "On second thought, why don't I eat your apple? If I can't have the real thing, at least I can nibble on nature's imitation."

"Pardon me if I don't stick around to watch," Jess mumbled. "It might make me feel like a voyeur to see you in flagrante delicto with an apple core." She jumped to her feet and brushed the bits of grass and twigs off her jeans. "It's time for me to get back to my painting."

The only sound she heard as she turned away was a faintly liquid crunch as the white, even line of Ethan's teeth bit cleanly into the apple.

Six

That night they baked apple pies. Ann Jenkins, Bill's wife, was happy to contribute a rolling pin, pie tins, aprons, and a cookbook to their efforts. Jess had to laugh at the sight of Ethan's elegant, muscular frame decked out in a voluminous, red-and-blue-flowered print apron. He tried to silence her giggles by brandishing the rolling pin and giving threatening snarls, but somehow that didn't have a sobering effect on Jess.

"Maybe you'd better take a look in the mirror before you start ridiculing *me*, Ms. Winslow," he suggested huffily. "You don't exactly look like something out of *Vogue* magazine yourself!"

And indeed she did not. The blue-and-white-checked fabric had been cinched in at her waist by wrapping the apron strings twice around, but still it bunched and sagged in a fairly comical way. Jess glanced down at herself, and her lips curved in a smile of nostalgic amusement.

"This reminds me of being a little girl helping my mother bake cookies. She always let me wear one of her aprons, even though it was miles too big for me." Jess was silent for a moment, remembering the big-eyed little girl who stood on a chair to stir the cookie dough and who had to be very careful to keep her long pigtails out of the mixing bowl. "I can still remember how proud and important I felt to be wearing my mother's apron," she said huskily, and then gave a self-conscious laugh as she realized Ethan was staring at her with an arrested look on his face.

Without a word he pulled her into his arms and placed a quick kiss on the very tip of her nose. "That's for looking so darn cute in that oversized apron," he said softly. "And *this*," he whispered, hugging her close so that his cheek rested against hers for a sweet, heady moment, "is for sharing that memory with me."

Only then did Jess realize what she'd just done. Without even thinking, as naturally as breathing, she'd given Ethan a personal glimpse into her past. And only that morning she'd been tied up in knots at the mere thought of telling him anything that might deepen their emotional intimacy. In just a few hours, her trust in him had been subtly strengthened. And she thought she knew why.

Almost any other man would have taken advantage of her temporary insanity in the apple orchard today. But not Ethan. Though it must have been obvious that her sexual response was surging out of control, he had kept his word and given her the chance to make a decision with her head instead of her hormones. And for having that kind of integrity, she had to respect him. The least she could do in return was share with him a few silly memories from her past.

So when Ethan oh, so casually slipped in a question about where she'd lived back when she was baking those cookies, Jess smiled and told him all about the ranch in northern California, near Red Bluff, where she'd grown up as an only child.

"Was it hard for you, being an only child?"

Jess pondered that for a minute. "Not really. My parents gave me plenty of love and attention, and even though I spent a lot of hours alone outdoors with just the hills and the sky for company, I never felt lonely. My head was always full of the things I'd seen, like sunsets, and wild flowers, and acres of grass rippling in the wind. I think that's why I started painting—I wanted to share all those special images that were in my head, and words just didn't seem adequate. I've felt that need ever since. Painting is the way I communicate the deepest part of me that words can't express."

Ethan was staring at her again, and Jess realized that she was telling him more than she'd meant to.

"You make it sound as if you've given up on other ways of communicating," he said slowly. "I wonder— are you afraid to try reaching out to someone in a more basic way? Your paintings are wonderfully intimate and revealing, but communication doesn't have to stop there, Jess. What have you got against real flesh-and-blood closeness?"

"I've got nothing against closeness," Jess snapped, "provided it's with the right person! I was just trying to explain why painting is so important to me. It's something I have to do or I don't feel whole. And I could never feel truly close to someone who didn't understand that part of me and take my work seriously."

There. Surely Ethan was intelligent enough to get the message in her last remark, and to realize why there might always be a limit to their friendship. And now it was definitely time to change the subject, before they got involved in another pointless argument.

"Do you like your apple pies with the apple skins left on or peeled off?" she asked abruptly.

"Who's doing the peeling?"

"You are." She gave him a knowing smile.

"Then, we'll leave the peels on. That'll add fiber to our diet, right?"

"Sounds like a good excuse to me. Please *do* remove the cores, though. We don't need that much fiber."

While Ethan sat down with knife, cutting board, and a bowl of freshly washed apples, Jess set to work mixing and rolling out pie crust. With the work divided up, it seemed scarcely any time at all before two cinnamon-and-sugar-sprinkled pies with fluted edges were carefully placed in the cabin's small oven.

Jess and Ethan shared the washing up as the pies baked and bubbled and filled the cabin with delicious aromas. When the kitchen area was tidy, they sat down to wait, occasionally sniffing the air in an exaggerated fashion.

"Somehow you've managed to get flour in your eyebrows," Jess informed Ethan with mock severity. Impulsively she reached up to brush away the faint dusting of white, and her fingertips unaccountably chose to linger there on the sleek, short-haired pelt of his brows, tracing the curving ridge of bone that lay beneath.

When he quizzically arched an eyebrow at her, the movement carried her finger upward on his forehead, making her intimately aware of the subtle tensing of his facial muscles. Her finger moved to the pulse at his temple, and the tiny, quickening throb of his flowing blood caused her own pulse to flicker with growing excitement. And then his eyes caught hers with a look that was intent and questioning. And hopeful.

Jess snatched her hand away, horrified at herself. She had no right to touch him like that, the situation between them being what it was. Her guilt deepened as she watched the glow in his eyes quickly fade.

"Sorry," she whispered, and then abruptly got up to take a quite unnecessary peek into the oven. Unnecessary for the pies, that is. Very necessary for her own peace of mind.

"One of these days, Jess, you and I are going to have a long, long talk," Ethan said quietly. "And you're going to tell me why you keep darting away from me like a frightened fawn."

"Ethan—"

"Don't worry. I'm not saying you have to tell me *now*. After all, I've got time to try to figure out the mystery for myself. I love a challenge." He gave her an enigmatic smile. "And you are definitely a challenge."

Oh, boy. All she needed was for Ethan to think of her as a *challenge*. "I'm going to try to round up some folks to help us eat these pies," she said briskly.

"Don't you trust yourself alone with me anymore?" he teased.

"What I don't trust myself with are two apple pies just out of the oven!" she shot back as she went out the door.

Bill and Ann were delighted to come, and a fair assortment of the guests in the other cabins were ready and willing to help sample apple pie and coffee. By the time the pies were ready, Jess's cabin was packed with a friendly crowd of strangers busily getting to know one another.

It was Ethan who took over making the second pot of coffee, and Jess found herself tuning out of the animated conversation going on around her as she watched him make his way from guest to guest, pouring refills of coffee and making each visitor feel specially welcomed with his smiling interest and easy humor. He's so damn charming, she thought, and couldn't help feeling a surge of pride and affection as well.

And then he caught her staring at him. Even from across the room, the look in his eyes made her blush, and she felt his gaze follow the waves of "wacky" pink color that swept down her throat and under the collar of her blouse. He gave her a knowing wink and a smile before bending to pour coffee for another guest.

By the time the convivial gathering had broken up, Jess was feeling very nervous at the thought of being alone with Ethan again. Today had been a roller-coaster ride of emotional and physical sensations, and it had left her confused. She had to face the fact that she was being drawn to Ethan against her will, like a meteor hurtling through space, destined for a fiery collision. She needed all her strength to fight this ever-accelerating gravitational pull that was tugging her headlong toward what might be destruction.

"I'll finish cleaning up," she said quickly as Ethan began to pick up the used paper plates and styrofoam cups left by their guests. "You go on home to bed."

"Whatever you say," he answered, but his voice was right behind her, and suddenly his arms were encircling her waist and drawing her back against the lean, muscled length of his legs and thighs. The quivering awareness that shot through her body made her go as taut as the bent string of a bow. Then, as Ethan's warmth enfolded her and his breath played softly on the skin of her neck, she felt herself crumbling into a soft, pliable mass of wants and desires that yearned for fulfillment.

And then, very gently, Ethan released her. "You see, I've finally learned my lesson. No kisses," he whispered as he stepped away. Jess felt a sudden wild, impossible urge to call to him, but, in her effort to hold back her body's instinctual cry, she bit her lip so hard, it bled. "Good night, Jess," he said softly, and the door closed after him.

She couldn't believe he was gone. Of course it was a relief. So why did she have this letdown feeling? Quickly she tidied up the cabin, and then she went to bed. But not to sleep. Her body couldn't seem to relax. First she lay on her right side. Then on her left. Then on her stomach. Then on her back. And then she tried all four positions over again.

She heard the creak of bedsprings from the other side of the wall, and knew that Ethan was also in bed. The thought of him lying there only a few feet away was not calculated to send her off to sleep any faster. She thought of his lips on her breasts in the apple orchard that afternoon, and her whole body felt hot and prickly beneath the sheet. She gave a sigh and turned onto her right side again.

When Ethan spoke to her through the wall, his voice sounded so close she almost imagined his head was on the pillow next to hers. "Feeling restless, Jess?" he asked, and she heard the thread of amusement in his voice. "I know a cure."

"I'll just bet you do. No, thanks, Ethan."

"Suit yourself. But I want you to know, you're welcome to do your tossing and turning over here in *my* bed anytime."

Jess greeted this offer with the silence it deserved. Fortunately, Ethan couldn't see the tiny smile dimpling her face.

"Jess? Are you thinking it over?"

" 'Fraid not, Ethan," she responded cheerfully.

"Then I'll have to try my second-best cure on you." The bed next door gave a loud protesting squeal as he slung himself out of it.

"Ethan! What are you doing?"

"You'll find out in just a minute," was his unreassuring reply. Jess sat up in bed and waited. Every muscle was tense as she tried to prepare herself for whatever surprise he was planning. And then she heard it.

Throaty and sweet, the strains of the Brahms "Lullaby," played on a clarinet, came drifting through the wall. Jess lay back against her pillow and let the gentle notes soothe her. She didn't even notice when the music changed to another flowing melody and then later to another. And she was completely unaware when the music stopped altogether, because by then she was sound asleep.

The next day marked the beginning of a sort of unspoken truce between them. Both Ethan and Jess were aware that their day in the apple orchard had set off so many sparks that the situation might explode at any minute. Jess was terrified at the thought, and she was determined to pull back and regroup her defenses. She was through being weak when it came to resisting Ethan Jamieson. What she wasn't prepared for was Ethan's own apparent change in attitude.

No doubt about it, he was handling her with the proverbial kid gloves. Once having rushed her to the brink of surrender, he now seemed content to bide his time. But he was watching her every second. Waiting. When he touched her, as he sometimes did, it was not in any obviously sexual way, but with warmth and affection. Still, he couldn't have failed to see what Jess tried so hard to hide—that the most impersonal physical contact between them had the power to stir her senses.

For a couple of days she was wary and suspicious, expecting him to pounce at any minute. But the easy, friendly intimacy of their hours together gradually lulled her once more. She forgot that she'd once tried to share as little of herself with him as possible. Now she told him things she'd never said aloud to anyone before. She forgot about the past, and she refused to think about the future. There was only the fragile sweetness of the present.

And the present seemed very sweet indeed one sunny noon hour as she lazed on the rocky crest of a very high hill, feeling contentedly drowsy after a brisk hike followed by a large and delicious picnic lunch.

"This view is fabulous," she murmured to Ethan, who was stretched out indolently beside her on the warm rock. Far below them the pines marched toward the coast, where the grassy headlands reached out like fingers into the sea. Mendocino itself looked like a wooden toy town, perched atop its faraway headland. Beyond was the blue ocean, with flecks of brilliant white where the breakers crashed against the rocks. Farther out still was the indecipherable line where sea merged into sky.

When Ethan made no reply to her comment, Jess turned to see if he'd fallen asleep. His eyes were open, but he seemed to take no pleasure in the scenic panorama spread before his brooding gaze.

"What's wrong?" Jess asked. "Are you thinking about one of those tragic shipwrecks that happened down there?"

"No." For a moment Jess thought he was going to leave it at that, without giving her an explanation. Then he sat up and clasped his tanned forearms around his denim-clad knees and spoke without meeting her eyes. "I was thinking how beautiful this view is, and I was regretting that my wife never got to see it. The climb would have been too much for her. I wanted to carry her up, but she wouldn't let me. She told me one invalid in the family was enough, and she didn't want me breaking my back trying to be Mr. Macho."

Jess took a great gulp of the pine-scented air. "I didn't know you were married," she said thickly.

"It's been six years since Gina died. The subject doesn't come up too often."

"I'm sorry. Would you prefer not to talk about it?"

"Actually, I've been wanting to tell you about her. It's the kind of thing friends should know about each other." There was only a slight inflection in his voice when he said "friends."

"How long were you married?" Jess asked hesitantly, half ashamed of her own curiosity. It had never occurred to her that Ethan might have been married once, and she was having to readjust her mental image of him.

"Five years. We met when we were still in college."

"And when did her illness start, the one that kept her from climbing the hill?"

"Gina was born with a serious heart condition. We knew all along that we were living on borrowed time, but that made every day we had together seem sweeter. She couldn't climb stairs or run races or go square dancing, but she managed to get more zest out of life than most healthy people do."

"She sounds very special. It must have been terri-

ble for you when she died, even if you were somewhat prepared for it."

"I wasn't prepared, even though I thought I was,"
he said grimly. "Toward the end, her condition suddenly deteriorated, until surgery was our only hope.
But the operation failed. That's when I realized I
had never truly believed she would die. I thought if I
could just protect her and take good enough care of
her, it would never happen. But it did. And I fell
apart. It took many weeks and a lot of support from
our friends and Gina's family before I started picking up the pieces again."

There was a long silence, and Jess felt choked by
all the useless words of sympathy she could have
spoken. But instinctively she knew Ethan wasn't
asking for her pity.

"More than a year went by before I was ready to
think about beginning any new relationships, and
then, when I did, they never seemed to last. It took
me a couple of years before I started to figure out
why. Unconsciously I'd been trying to recreate my
relationship with Gina by getting involved with
women who made me feel protective. I was a sucker
for the fragile, helpless type."

He twisted his lips in a self-deprecating smile. "It
was all pretty crazy. Because no matter how protective
I felt of Gina, she was never a helpless person. Though
she was physically weak, emotionally she was one very
strong, plucky lady. In the end, she had a hell of a
lot more courage than I did. So how could a truly
weak person have replaced what I had with her?"

He went on without waiting for an answer. "But my
biggest mistake was in trying to recreate the past in
the first place. My memories of Gina will always be
part of me, but I couldn't be happy with a *copy* of that
relationship. When I finally realized that, I started
looking for what I'd needed all along—a brand-new
original, not a substitute." He paused, and took a deep
breath. "The only problem was, the woman I was
looking for turned out to be very hard to find. I got
discouraged. Once or twice I even found myself falling

into the same old trap of trying to form a relationship based on my misguided attempts to help someone."

"Like Beryl?" Jess asked softly.

"Exactly. But that's one mistake I'll never make again." He turned suddenly and looked directly at Jess, but now she was the one staring out at the distant horizon without speaking. The thought of trying to become that "brand-new original" woman Ethan was looking for was suddenly dangerously tempting. The more time she spent with him, the more deeply she cared for this funny, complex, and *damnably* attractive man. He deserved to find a woman to make him happy again. But that woman couldn't be Jess. It would never work. Not once they went back to the city and took up the divergent paths of their professional lives.

"Thank you for telling me, Ethan," she said at last, giving him a warm, tender smile. "It makes me feel more truly your friend, now that you've shared this with me. I just wish there were some way I could express how sorry I am that you had to lose Gina. Words seem so inadequate."

"Jess—" he began hesitantly, but just then a sudden gust of wind threatened to whisk away the remnants of their picnic lunch, much to Jess's relief, since it gave her a chance to change the subject.

"Brrr! The wind's getting chilly up here! Don't you think it's time we started back down?"

Ethan shrugged in resignation. "Whatever you say, Jess. I'm in no hurry."

If there was a double meaning in that, Jess chose to ignore it. She wasn't ready for any complications to disrupt the peace and companionship she'd enjoyed with Ethan these last few days. Of course this halcyon interlude couldn't last forever, but that was no reason to hurry it on its way by looking for innuendos in everything. Soon they were joking as lightheartedly as usual, and Jess congratulated herself that she'd maneuvered round a rather tricky moment.

But later she thought about the tragedy in Ethan's

past, and felt confused at the ache of tenderness that overwhelmed her. His pain had the power to hurt her, it seemed. How odd that their friendship had grown so deep and close after all, without her even being fully aware of it until now.

The following morning Jess awoke to the sounds of the first storm of the winter rainy reason. All day long, shrieking winds and sheets of rain buffeted the little cabin, and Jess could hear the waves growling below the cliffs and gnawing at the headlands. Any excursion with Ethan would have been impractical, so she worked alone in the chilly cabin, longing for the light and color and companionship of the last few days. She didn't know what Ethan found to do, except that for a while he made very mournful music next door on his clarinet.

When hunger pangs began to inform her that it was time to stop work for the day, Jess discovered she was not looking forward to the long evening ahead. The cabin was drafty and cheerless. Her tiny refrigerator offered up only aging cottage cheese, limp lettuce, and a boiled egg as possibilities for her evening meal. Her muscles were cramped from bending over her work, and the fury of the storm outside made her feel very lost and alone. In fact she was dangerously close to feeling downright sorry for herself.

When Ethan's knock came at the door she felt a rushing uplift of spirits. "Good, you haven't started cooking yet," he said.

"I'm afraid there's not much *to* cook." She laughed, and realized it was the first time she'd laughed all day. How good it felt!

"Even better! That means you're completely at my mercy. You'll have to eat my cooking even if I burn the steaks."

"Did you say steaks?"

"You heard me. Be there in five minutes." He turned to go, and then added, "I've got a fire going, so you won't need quite so many sweaters as you've got on now."

"A fire!" she exclaimed, but he was gone. She decided to take him at his word, and quickly removed several bulky layers she'd been huddling in for warmth. Shivering, she slipped into a silky blouse, draped one sweater across her shoulders, and hurried in search of the promised fire.

It was a glorious fire, crackling cheerfully in the old stone fireplace that dominated the room. "I never even noticed you had a fireplace!" she said. And then she remembered that she hadn't been in his cabin since that first night.

"You know, for an artist you're pretty unobservant sometimes," he teased her. "I can understand your not picking up on a minor detail like a fireplace the one time you were here, since on that occasion the lighting was rather dim and you were busy fighting off a raving lunatic. But that chimney outside is hard to miss!"

"I never made the connection," Jess confessed. "It just didn't occur to me that where there's a chimney, there must be a fireplace. But now I'm jealous, because my half of the cabin doesn't have one!"

"You're welcome to warm yourself by my fire any time," he told her, and she felt her cheeks grow hot at his suggestive smile.

They ate steak and salad, seated on cushions in front of the fire, and it was so warm that Jess soon slipped off her sweater. She felt flushed from the heat and from the red wine they were drinking. The throbbing, interminable beat of the rain against the cabin roof sealed them into a warm, firelit cocoon together. And within that cocoon, Jess felt the stirrings of change. Not only the weather had altered, but something in herself as well. She was no longer content with things the way they were.

She stared at Ethan in hungry fascination—how his skin glowed in the firelight, how each lean line of him from jaw to thigh was strong and perfect, with a clean, hard beauty that made her ache inside.

The way his supple fingers curved around his glass of wine awakened the memory of how those same fingers had once curved to cup her own flesh.

Lying back against the cushions, Jess felt dizzy and confused with the heat of her thoughts. Then her eyes met Ethan's, and she trembled at the molten fires of desire suddenly blazing there. A surge of rebellion boiled up inside her. Why should she have to fight this piercing need, this raging inferno within herself? Why should she deny herself and Ethan for the sake of a few scruples?

Of course she knew darn well that whatever they shared together couldn't endure beyond these few days in Mendocino. The man in jeans and plaid woolen shirt who lounged beside her in front of the fire was someone she'd come to regard as a friend. She trusted *him*—this man who'd kept his promises, and who'd shared so many hours of laughter and companionable silence. But she didn't trust that other man he would become once his vacation was over. That hawk-eyed, hard-jawed, determined man in the three-piece suit. That man who was single-mindedly caught up in the high-pressure business of expanding the reputation and sales of the Fiori chain of stores.

No, she couldn't make any lasting commitment to *that* man. But why should that stop her from sharing a temporary joy with this warm, tender man at her side? They had wanted each other for so long, and just because their relationship had no future was no reason why they shouldn't have tonight. Surely they were entitled to that! Didn't the very strength of this mindless, searing attraction between them give them the right to some sort of satisfaction? Whom would they be hurting? *Each other*, a tiny voice answered, but Jess was in no mood to pay attention.

When Ethan reached out to rest his hands on her shoulders, she couldn't resist savoring the sensuous caress of his thumb against her collarbone. Slowly she turned her head and pressed her mouth against his hand, exulting when she felt the tremor that went through him at her gesture of acceptance.

"*Now* may I kiss you, Jess?" he asked with breathless intensity, and they were both aware that he was asking for much more than just one kiss.

"Yes, please, Ethan," she breathed. Instantly his lips melded with her pliant mouth, and his tongue pressed between her lips like a flicker of flame, igniting her blood with deeper passion. It was a long, burning kiss that exploded with the force of all their pent-up yearning. Before it was over, Ethan's hands were unbuttoning her blouse, and then Jess gasped as she felt his hot kisses pressed in ardent clusters along the fullness of her breasts where they met the lacy edge of her bra. His fingers found the clasp to that, and he cupped her breasts in his palms while his tongue circled over her flesh, moving ever closer to her upturned nipples, which burned for his moist caress. Jess buried her face in the woodsmoke-scented darkness of his hair, feeling herself go mad with pleasure.

The moment when his mouth took full possession was so intense that Jess gave a broken cry like the sound that a charred piece of wood makes falling deeper into the fire. She felt wrapped in flame from head to toe. Soon Ethan's mouth returned to hers with an urgency not to be denied, and his hands were deft and quick as they loosened her heavy plait of hair so it tumbled in luxuriant waves across her shoulders. He slipped her blouse and bra down her arms and laid them aside, and then drew back to gaze at her flushed face, and at her hair, flaming in the firelight against her gleaming white nakedness.

"I've dreamed of seeing you like this," he murmured hoarsely, and Jess knew that she had dreamed of it too. Her seeking, hungry hands had parted his plaid woolen shirt in order to wander lovingly over his smooth, heated flesh. She wanted to possess his entire body with her kisses.

Then Ethan took her in his arms once more, and she felt the rough hair of his chest pressed against her breasts. He murmured her name and kissed her, and his hands moved over her waist and crept down the blue-jeaned length of her thigh. The tantalizing pressure of his fingertips sent a tongue of flame licking along her inner thighs to the core of her desire, and Jess was overcome with wanting. She craved his hard, vibrant possession. Her hips arched with an involuntary quiver as Ethan slid open her zipper and slipped his strong fingers inside. Jess felt her inner flesh turn to quicksilver delight, rippling with arousal in response to the rhythmic, intimate stroking of Ethan's hand.

"Please, please . . ." she gasped, and then with an inarticulate groan she reached for the belt buckle of his jeans. Her hands shook as she tugged at his clothes, pulling the rough denim quickly down over his lean, smooth hips. With wild abandon she let her fingers and mouth trail in the wake of his clothing, caressing each newly exposed expanse of muscled thigh and calf. The downy softness of his body hair was like an answering caress that teased at every aroused nerve in her fingertips and swollen lips.

Ethan's soft groans of pleasure at her lovemaking mounted rapidly in intensity, until suddenly he took her by the wrists and drew her hard against him.

"No more, Jess! Or I won't be any good for what comes next." He gave a very shaky laugh. "My God, you're even more woman than I dreamed you'd be."

"Is that good or bad?" she murmured breathlessly, nibbling at his collarbone.

"It's wonderful. *You're* wonderful." There was such a blazing warmth of feeling in his tawny eyes that Jess was startled. "I feel like the luckiest man in the world," he said huskily, and Jess experienced first a thrill of happiness and then a tremor of disquiet. This was supposed to be just a holiday fling, yet Ethan sounded like— But suddenly there was no time for second thoughts, as the tempo of their lovemaking quickened once more.

Ethan locked his mouth against hers for a deep,

pulsating kiss, while his hands quickly eased her jeans off her body so that she lay naked against the cushions. The firelight flickered over them both, burnishing their skins to coppery gold, as if they were precious metal, softened by heat and ready to be welded together. For a long moment Ethan held himself poised above her, and their passion-darkened eyes met in a look of mutual urgency. Then, with an indrawn breath, he lowered his hot flesh to hers.

Never had Jess felt so ripe for the moment of mutual possession, and never had that moment been so electrically, joltingly satisfying as it was when Ethan entered her. But that instant of satisfaction was swept away by the sharp, explosive craving that grew more intense with every second that their bodies were joined in rhythmic fusion. And then that, too, was gone in a great inner shower of sparks, a white-hot fountain of joyous sensation that erupted over and over, and then left her floating mindlessly earthward.

She discovered herself clinging to Ethan's shoulders, just as a long, ragged cry was ripped from deep within him. The convulsive shuddering of his body was followed by a series of quivering aftershocks, and then he dropped his head against Jess's shoulder and lay still.

The golden peace of pure contentment blanketed them like liquid amber. Jess thought she would preserve this moment in her memory forever, because tonight was the closest to perfection that life had ever come for her.

And then Ethan spoke, in a voice still breathless and uneven from their act of love, and his words completely shattered the perfect memory she'd planned to keep.

"I love you, Jess Winslow," he said.

Seven

"You don't mean that," she said quickly.

"But I do." He lifted himself on his elbows and cupped her face with his hands, gazing at her with a tender, intimately searching look that terrified her. "I love you very much."

No! She wanted to scream it aloud. Don't let it be true! But of course it was true. And only a fool could have failed to guess the strength of Ethan's feelings long before this. Or worse than a fool—a selfish woman who would rather deceive herself than face the truth, because the truth would have required her to listen to her conscience and deny herself tonight's ecstasy. Because it was wrong to take a man's love and give back only sexual passion, even when that passion was the most magically intense she'd ever known.

She couldn't forgive her own willful blindness. All the clues had been there, in Ethan's every word and look, and in every touch and caress of his lovemaking, but she had refused to see. She had let herself believe only what she wanted to believe. Now there was no alternative but to hurt him, and hurt him badly, when it was the last thing she wanted to do.

"Ethan." Her voice was thick and strangled. Each word was an ordeal, and she turned her head away so she wouldn't have to see the expression in his eyes while she told him. "I don't love you back."

She felt him go tense against her. There was a long, horrible silence before he spoke at last.

"I don't believe you."

"What?" It was the last thing she had expected him to say.

"I said, I don't believe you. I think you do love me."

"No!" Her cry was desperate. "This is all a mistake. I *wanted* you tonight, Ethan, so I never stopped to think that it might mean more to you than it did to me. I'm sorry." She forced herself to look at him once more. "It was wrong, and it won't happen again."

"Dammit, Jess! There was nothing wrong or mistaken about our making love! And it's definitely going to happen again. You know as well as I do how *right* it was!"

"You mean physically. But emotionally I cheated you, Ethan. I never meant to, but that won't make it any easier to forgive."

"I don't feel cheated." He spoke very quietly, but the rough-soft texture of his voice was full of intimate memories of the passion they had just shared. His eyes blazed with it, and with fierce, tender knowledge of the woman who lay naked beneath him. "I don't feel cheated at all."

"But you *should*," Jess protested weakly. "Unless it's really enough for you that I wanted you physically, without loving you."

"When are you going to stop kidding yourself, Jess?"

"What do you mean?" But even before he answered, she knew what he was thinking.

"I mean, why is it so impossible for you to admit that you love me?"

"But I don't! You're the one who's kidding yourself!" An inexplicable feeling of panic seized her by the throat and forced its way into her chest. "Why must you make this so much harder for both of us by

deluding yourself? You are a wonderful, charming man, and I like you very much. You are also the best lover I ever had. But I don't love you. I can't love you. Please just accept that."

"How *can* I accept it, when I hear love in your voice and see it in your eyes?" His voice was ragged with emotion. "I know the difference between love and lust, Jess, so don't tell me you only *want* me! You didn't see your own face tonight when we made love. I did. Believe me, you love me."

She stared up at him with wide, frightened green eyes. Her thoughts were in chaos, as wave after wave of inexplicable fear rolled over her. Like a tiny insect seeking just a taste of honey, she suddenly found herself ensnared in a sweet, sticky bondage from which there was no obvious escape.

"Why are you so afraid of loving me?" he asked. "I swear that you don't need to be. I won't hurt you, ever."

Jess couldn't answer him. No, *he* wouldn't hurt her, but what about that man in the three-piece suit?

"I'm willing to wait," he said gently. "Someday you'll be ready to say you love me, and I can wait . . . for *that*. But don't make me wait for this." And his mouth came down on hers as hotly, as sweetly, as the sun's embrace on a summer morning.

"But it's not fair to you," she protested, turning her mouth away and struggling in his arms. "I'll never feel more than a physical attraction for you."

"Call it whatever you want. Pretend it's only lust if that makes you feel better," he whispered against the rose-petal softness of her earlobe, while his hand stroked caressingly down her throat and cupped each breast in turn. Jess felt her determination crumbling as his lips, teeth, and tongue played seductively in the curves and hollows of her ear.

"Are you sure you want this?" she asked him urgently. She knew she ought to continue trying to protect him from his own delusions about her feelings, but somehow her objections didn't sound very convincing anymore. Not even to her.

"You've got to be kidding," he drawled, and his mouth quirked into a gently mocking smile. "Of course I want it, you idiot. Don't you?" His eyes held hers for a long, questioning moment, while Jess struggled to force herself to say the lie, to tell Ethan that she did *not*, in fact, want to make love with him again. But she waited too long.

"Will this help you decide?" he asked. And then his lips were warm on the hard pink buds of her nipples, awakening again the swelling seeds of her desire to sprout and send up a lush, primeval growth, a jungle of sensual need that crowded out all rational thought.

It was as if her flesh had lain empty and fallow, replenishing itself in readiness for his touch, instead of having once already that night been reaped of a rich, bounteous harvest of passion.

"Yes, I want it," she gasped. "I want *you*." And she moaned as his hand traveled slowly down her belly.

"Then, the words don't matter," he murmured huskily, finding the warm, moist place where every touch of his fingers caused her flesh to blossom with pleasure. "Not when I can feel you loving me like this."

Vaguely Jess knew she should protest once more, and tell him that this was no proof of love. But she didn't want to breathe one word that might make Ethan stop the wonderful things he was doing to her. She couldn't have stood it if he stopped now.

But Ethan had no thought of stopping. Hovering just above her, he moved the hard shaft of his maleness in teasing, playful strokes along the soft skin of her inner thighs. Delicately as a butterfly seeking nectar at the heart of a flower, he moved lightly against her. Each tantalizing, gossamer stroke of his probing flesh was such sweet torment that Jess cried out, partly with pleasure and partly with frustration.

In a gesture of wordless pleading, her hands pressed

against his muscled buttocks as she urged him closer and arched herself to meet him. Ethan's hands dropped to her hips and brought her up hard against him in one quick, fluid motion. Jess gasped in delight as her body opened to him like the petals of a flower opening to the sun.

Minutes later, it was over. What had begun as a gentle stirring of the senses and grown into a powerful, striving need, now burst into riotous blossom within her as she and Ethan found complete union. There was a moment of utter splendor and perfect beauty before the bright, fleeting bloom of passion began to fade, as all flowers must.

But even while flowers fade, their fruits are forming, full of ripening promise for the future. While Jess and Ethan lay nestled together, floating on the edge of that deep, satisfying sleep all contented lovers know, the truth came to Jess at last. Ethan was perfectly right. She did love him after all.

What a fool she'd been, to think that something as potent and intense as the physical attraction between them could exist without emotional consequences. She had flung herself into the heart of a flame when she made love with Ethan, so how could she expect to emerge unchanged, untouched? And she should never have underestimated the power of his love to call forth an answering love in her.

This feeling wasn't just the fragile, temporary bloom of desire, which could easily be plucked from her life when the time came to say good-bye. This was a love that had been growing for many days, unknown to her. Already it had taken root deep in her heart, and tonight she had recklessly given it the chance to flower and bear fruit. Now it promised an abundant harvest of grief.

Jess felt her body turn cold with fear. Even where her skin lay against the warm, solid flesh of Ethan's gently breathing chest, the inner chill of her thoughts took over, and she felt imprisoned by his arms. A man like Ethan could destroy her.

He wouldn't do it intentionally, of course. But just

by being who he was, he had the power to enslave her emotions and make her helpless with love. And what would happen to the artist struggling within her once she was under the spell of that *other* Ethan? If his attitudes toward art and money turned out to be anything like Cliff's, it would be a living nightmare.

The drive to create and communicate as a painter was an essential part of Jess, and it took long hours of concentration and hard work. Painting was so absorbing and important to her that she had been known to ignore ringing phones and forget dinner engagements and incinerate casseroles left in the oven while she worked. Could Ethan understand and respect her work enough to accept that kind of thing as an occupational hazard? Would he take her work seriously even though it was financially unproductive? She was afraid the answer was no.

And would he start putting her down with disparaging remarks, the way Cliff had done? Would he apply the same subtle and not-so-subtle pressures on her to give up painting? She couldn't go through that again—being torn apart by the conflict between her need to please the man she loved and her need to be true to herself. That was no way to live.

She'd had the strength to walk away from her engagement to Cliff when their relationship became a destructive one. But could she do that with Ethan? His lovemaking tonight had shown her how impossible it would be. Ethan would possess her, body and soul. With only a kiss, or a word, or a smile, he could mold her like clay until nothing was left of the woman she'd once been.

Panic throbbed in every beat of her pulses now. Immediate escape began to seem like the only answer. She must get away while she still had the strength to leave. She must go *now*. That thought alone obsessed her as Jess began to ease herself out of Ethan's firm hold. She was afraid to breathe for fear of waking him, and she flinched as he gave a muffled sigh at being left with mere emptiness in his arms where she had lain. Keeping alert for any change in the deep, reassuring rhythm of his breathing, Jess put out a trembling hand to grope for her clothes in the near-darkness.

Did it really have to be this way? she asked herself as the mist of terror receded slightly and a few doubts crept in. Wasn't it wrong to run away without even giving Ethan a chance? Maybe . . . But the risk was too great. If she lay next to Ethan till morning and shared the ritual of waking together, it would be too late to run. She'd never find the strength of will to leave him, not even if all her worst fears about him were true.

A fierce ache of love gripped her as she bent over his sleeping form, trying to say a silent good-bye though she was almost overwhelmed by the temptation to stay. It would have been heaven to let herself love Ethan and be loved by him in return. But if the price of that earthly paradise was the loss of her vocation as an artist, that was the one price Jess couldn't pay. It would have been like selling her soul.

Stealthily she crossed the floor and let herself out into the cold, wet night. The wind had died down, but the rain still poured relentlessly from the skies. She had never felt so alone as she did now, in the process of deliberately cutting herself off from the one person who mattered more to her than anyone else in the world.

Her own cabin was like a damp, chilly cave. But that didn't matter. She wouldn't be here long. Working as swiftly as caution allowed, Jess gathered up her belongings and began to cram them into suitcases and boxes. Every slight creak or click or bump that she made seemed to echo ominously in the silent room. She knew only too well how clearly every sound could be heard on the other side of the wall, and she breathed more easily once she was outside again.

The short, but numerous, trips from the cabin to the car seemed to take twice as long as usual in the dark. The rain had immediately soaked through her sweater and trickled miserably down her spine. At least the paintings she carried were in no danger of getting wet—some were wrapped in her own raincoat, others in heavy tarpaulin.

During the past twenty-four hours the dusty parking lot had been transformed into a giant mud puddle. Old Betsy was up to her hubcaps in murky brown water, which turned out to be colder on each succeeding trip. More than once Jess almost slipped and fell, but miraculously her precious artwork reached the car unscathed. The same could not be said for Jess herself. She was so wet by now that there seemed little point in retrieving her raincoat once she'd loaded her paintings into the car, so she hurried back to the cabin without it. She had a couple more armloads of things to carry to the car before she could be on her way.

Her mud-soaked sneakers squelched on the plank walk as she approached the cabin, and Jess slowed her steps to a furtive tiptoeing. Very quietly she turned the knob and opened her door. Still on tiptoe, she crossed the floor to the table where her remaining belongings were stacked. Carefully she shone the beam of her flashlight around the room, checking for any object she might have overlooked in her frantic haste. And there it was, of course—her pale green bathrobe hanging ghostlike from a hook on the bathroom door. Would it fit into the already-bulging suitcase? Preoccupied with this concern, Jess forgot to be cautious as she darted over to the bathroom door and back.

The combination of speed and muddy feet on the uncarpeted linoleum floor was disastrous. Jess went into an uncontrolled skid that flung her off balance and carried her full-tilt against the rickety table where she'd piled her gear. Suitcase, art supplies, a box of kitchen paraphernalia, and the old table itself crashed to the floor with a noise like thunder. And as if that weren't enough to wake up every sleeper in the immediate vicinity, an involuntary shriek was torn from Jess's lungs as she went sprawling amid the wreckage.

There was no time to lie whimpering with pain or panting with terror, though Jess felt strongly inclined to do both. But she knew from the sounds coming through the wall that Ethan was now awake and calling her name. She didn't have a second to lose.

Snatching her purse, flashlight, and suitcase, but abandoning her other possessions, Jess sped out the door and ran, limping, toward the parking lot. Her reasons for running didn't matter anymore—she was operating on pure panic now.

Just as she reached the shallow lake of muddy water where Old Betsy waited, Jess heard Ethan's shout behind her in the darkness. He had no flashlight, and she hoped that would slow him down but not cause him to break a leg.

Her own limbs were in some danger of that fate as she recklessly tried to run through water that swirled at mid-calf height over a treacherous bed of mud. The good luck that had kept her and her paintings from falling into a cold mud-bath on her first trips across the parking lot had definitely run out. This time she did fall. Not just once, but several times.

Jess was sobbing with fear and exhaustion by the time she wrestled her muddy suitcase into the luggage compartment at the front of the little VW. Her hands were cold and slippery with mud as she struggled to open the car door. She collapsed sideways on the seat behind the wheel, and only the thought of Ethan closing in on her gave her the strength to swing her legs inside the car and shut the door.

Her hands were about as useful as two mud-caked blocks of wood as she pawed frantically through the filthy, water-soaked contents of her purse in search of her car keys. At last the key ring was in her grasp, rattling like a pair of castanets as her body trembled and her fingers fumbled for the right key. She gave a sigh of relief when at last the key was inserted in the ignition. Her relief was short-lived. After so many hours of sitting neglected in such decidedly damp weather, Old Betsy felt completely justified in showing her temperamental side. The engine sputtered but would not catch.

"Don't do this to me, Bets!" Jess pleaded desperately. "Come on, old girl, you know you can do it," she coaxed as she tried again.

Still the old car refused to start.

"If you fail me now I will personally haul you to the junk yard and give a standing ovation while they flatten you into scrap metal! *Start*, dammit! Or *else*."

Whether this threat did the trick, or whether some more mechanical process was at work, Jess would never know. And she didn't care. All that mattered to her was that Old Betsy's engine finally roared into life. The old girl sounded rough, cranky, and uncertain, but all Jess wanted was enough juice to get out of there. The rest of her life could take care of itself if only she could survive the next half hour.

She eased the car into first gear and switched on the headlights. Their harsh glare reflected off the dark water, giving sudden visual substance to shapes that had been invisible in the blackness of the night. Trees with twisted branches. The low, hulking forms of the other cars in the flooded lot. And the shape that leaped most vividly into view—Ethan. He was only ten feet away and moving closer. For an instant Jess simply gripped the wheel and stared at him, overwhelmed.

He hadn't stopped to dress before dashing out after her, except to pull on a pair of jeans that were now so soaked with rain and mud that they clung to his slim hips like a second skin. It was obvious from the rapid rise and fall of his chest that he'd been running very hard. The muscles of his naked shoulders and arms glistened with rain, and rain ran in rivulets down his face. The rugged boniness of his features stood out starkly in the glare of the headlights. His dark hair was plastered to his skull and his eyes were like twin pools of darkness. He looked shocked and furious and very determined.

As he moved toward her with the lithe dark grace of a stalking panther, Jess felt the instinct to flee take complete hold of her. She slammed her foot on the gas and released the clutch. Old Betsy lurched forward with an unladylike belch, and Jess hung on to the wheel for dear life as the car's tires slithered and spun in the mire.

Ethan sprang at the car as if he intended to block her escape with his own body. He seized the door handle on her side and tried to wrench it open, shouting at Jess the whole time. She shuddered. Thank goodness it was locked.

But something was terribly wrong. Why wasn't she moving? Jess floored the gas pedal so hard the engine shrieked and the tires whirred, but Old Betsy stubbornly refused to budge. The sharp odor of gasoline fumes filled the air. Jess moaned in despair as she realized she was hopelessly stuck. Her frantic efforts to pull free were only digging the tires deeper and deeper into the mud.

But that was not the final catastrophe. Even if she couldn't drive away, at least she was locked in a safe cocoon where Ethan couldn't touch her. Or so she thought. And then he yanked open the unlocked passenger door and plopped himself in beside her, breathing heavily.

"No," Jess whimpered dazedly. "I was sure that door was locked." And she began to cry, helplessly, silently, with tears cascading down her face. He'd defeated her. Or maybe she'd defeated herself, and that was worse.

Ethan stared at her in silence, and whatever words he'd planned to hurl at her remained unsaid. Finally he reached out to take her gently by the shoulders, but Jess twisted wildly away.

"Don't touch me!" she cried. "I can't bear it!" She put her arms up on the steering wheel and buried her face against them, giving in to hysterical, convulsive sobs that shook her whole body.

If she had looked up, she would have seen the bruised expression around Ethan's mouth as he withdrew his hands. His eyes were hard and glazed-looking as he stared unseeingly out the windshield into the rain, listening to the tormented sobs of the woman next to him. Since she wouldn't accept his comforting, he had three choices. He could walk away and leave her to it. Or he could use violence and try to snap her out of it—a quick slap or a hard shaking might do the trick. Or he could sit here and wait and endure while the storm of emotion ran its course. Being the man he was, Ethan chose to wait. And endure.

Gradually Jess's sobs began to subside, and she was left feeling weaker and colder than she'd ever felt before. The cold was like an ache that penetrated to the deepest part of her. She sensed Ethan's presence next to her in the car, and wondered what he thought of her now. Perhaps he wouldn't want her anymore, after seeing her in the middle of a crying fit like this. Men were easily scared off by such scenes. *That* would certainly solve her problems! But somehow it wasn't a comforting thought.

She peered sideways at him through the tangle of hair covering her tear-swollen face. He was hunched over with the cold, hugging his bare arms against his wet chest. He was shivering, just a little. And she couldn't read the expression on his face.

"You're cold," she said inanely. What *did* you say to a man after fleeing from his bed and then sobbing hysterically when he caught up with you after a mad pursuit through a giant mud puddle? What did you say to a man who claimed to love you, when you loved him back but didn't dare let him know?

"Yeah," he grunted, and a ghost of a smile twisted his lips. "You look a little chilly yourself. Why don't you turn the heater on?"

"It doesn't work. You'd better get back to the cabin before you catch pneumonia," she said shakily, looking away.

"I'm waiting for you." His voice was very gentle, but with an undercurrent of rock-hard determination.

"No!" Jess snapped wearily. "I've got to get away. You've got to let me go."

"I'll let you go, if that's what you want. But not tonight. Not when you're worn out and upset and half dead with cold. Not when the weather's like this, and you might run into mud slides or washed-out roads."

"You don't understand! I've got to go *now*, or it might be too late." She couldn't bear his concern for her, his tenderness.

"You're darn right I don't understand!" he said fiercely. "You haven't given me a clue about why you're so determined to run away from the best thing that ever happened to either of us!" And then his voice grew quieter. "But I do see that you're scared as hell that I'll somehow persuade you to stay and give our relationship a chance. Well, you don't have to worry."

"What do you mean?"

"I'll stay away from you, Jess." His voice was bleak. "I won't even try to change your mind. You'll be safe here. You don't have to run."

"I don't believe you." Her lips felt so numb with cold she could scarcely speak.

"Damn you! How the hell do you think it makes me feel to see you in a panic like this, and to know that for some reason *I'm* the one you're afraid of?" His words burst out in a painful shout that cracked and broke with emotion. He paused a moment to regain control before going on.

"I remember when I was a boy, I once tried to rescue a bird with a broken wing. Its feathers were all wet and bedraggled, and it trembled so hard I thought its heart would give out. I only wanted to help, but that damn silly bird went crazy with terror every time I came near. In fact, that little bird was so afraid of me it broke its neck trying to fly away through a windowpane, even though its wing was so crippled it could scarcely flutter off the ground."

"I'm sorry, Ethan," Jess whispered, and they both knew she wasn't just expressing sympathy for the long-ago death of a frightened bird. "You mustn't blame yourself."

"I don't. The point of the story is, Jess, that I learned something from the experience. It didn't cure me of trying to rescue fallen sparrows, I'm afraid. But it did teach me that I couldn't play God. I can't force birds or people to accept my help, or my love. It's not my place to decide for others what's best for them." He sighed. "If a woman as strong and intelligent as you, Jess, decides she has to run away from a relationship, then I have to respect that decision, because I respect you. So you can trust me when I promise that you don't have to run any farther than this parking lot to escape from me. Now, will you please come back to the cabin before we both succumb to hypothermia?"

"Okay." She was too cold and tired to do any more arguing, or any more running either, for that matter. "What's hypo—hypothum—?" Her mouth couldn't seem to form the unfamiliar syllables, and her chattering teeth didn't help any.

"Hypothermia." Ethan leaned over and turned off the headlights, took the key out of the ignition, and unlocked her door before getting out and wading around the car to help her out. Jess found she didn't resent his assistance, since she felt oddly clumsy and light-headed. And she was so exhausted she didn't even protest when Ethan picked her up and started carrying her.

"Hypothermia," he continued, as if he were reciting to her from a textbook, "occurs when the body loses heat faster than it produces it, which is especially likely to happen when clothing becomes too wet to insulate the body properly. The early symptoms of hypothermia are slurred speech, fatigue, loss of dexterity, and uncontrollable shivering."

"Oh, dear!" Jess exclaimed weakly. "What happens then?"

"Nothing, if you're able to get warm and dry again. But if your body temperature keeps falling, you become disoriented and lethargic, and eventually you go to sleep and you don't wake up. It's called dying of exposure."

Jess would have shuddered if her whole body hadn't been shaking already. "You're not saying that could happen to us? It's not even *near* freezing out here!" she protested.

"Freezing has nothing to do with it. If your body can't maintain a certain internal temperature, it stops functioning and you die. And that happens long before the blood ices over in your veins, believe me. It could easily have happened tonight."

"Must you be so g-ghoulish about it?"

"I'm trying to scare a little common sense into you, Jess! Next time you run off in the pouring rain, wear a wool sweater and a raincoat! Carry an umbrella! I'm serious, Jess!" he bellowed as she started to giggle nervously. "And if you do get wet, for God's sake don't drive off in a car with a broken heater!"

He was panting now, from the exertion of carrying her and scolding her at the same time, and Jess was suddenly conscious of the slippery smoothness of his shoulders where she clung to him. The sound of his labored breathing and the feel of his moist, naked skin were unbearably intimate in the vast, rain-drenched night that surrounded them. From out across the headland, Jess was suddenly aware of the relentless crashing of ocean waves against the rocks, and for an instant she felt as if she and Ethan were the only warm-blooded creatures in an alien world of cold, wet darkness. It wasn't fair. How could she stop loving him if she was forced to endure this closeness and experience this bond of shared vulnerability? She twisted in his arms.

"Put me down. I can walk now," she said quickly. "Please," she added when Ethan hesitated. He set her carefully on her feet, and she stumbled along at his side, thinking of the promise he had given her and wondering if that could possibly be enough to save her from losing herself completely to him.

"What would you have done," she asked suddenly, "if I hadn't agreed to come back to the cabin with you? Would you have sat there waiting until we both turned into basket cases?"

"Of course not. I was just about ready to throw you over my shoulder like a wet sack of potatoes and haul you back kicking and screaming. Luckily you wised up in time to avoid that fate."

She stopped abruptly, but Ethan took her by the arm and kept her moving. "What about all your fine words back there about not forcing your help on people?" she wanted to know. "Didn't you say something about not interfering with other people's decisions? Or was that little bird episode just a story you invented for my benefit?"

"Did you expect me to leave you to die, Jess?" he countered grimly. "Would that have made you happy?"

"It wouldn't have come to that," she said in a faltering voice.

"How the hell do you know? Hypothermia victims are usually the worst judges of their own condition, and you're no exception. You'd better start taking Mother Nature more seriously."

"I do. Believe me, I do!" Jess said with fervor. It was good old Mother Nature that had gotten her into this mess in the first place!

"Good," he said. "And in case you're still wondering, I did mean what I said earlier, but there are limits. You're free to live your own life, but I'm not going to stand by while you kill yourself. Understood?" He shone the flashlight over toward her, waiting for an answer, and Jess finally nodded.

They plodded on in silence. Jess ached with cold and weariness, and it required an effort of will to keep putting one foot in front of the other, over and over again. Then at last her feet squelched heavily on the boards of the plank walk. Soon they stopped in front of a door that Ethan opened, and he pushed her inside.

"You get out of those wet clothes and into the shower," he ordered. "I'll get the fire going again."

Startled, Jess looked up and saw the fireplace. The cushions still lay in front of it, still bearing the imprints where two bodies had pressed so ardently in lovemaking. Ethan's shirt still lay on the floor.

Suddenly she hurt so much inside she thought her chest would explode.

"I'd rather shower in my own cabin, if you don't mind," she said.

"But I do mind," he said wearily. "There's no fireplace in your room, and if you took it into your head to lock yourself in, you might not get warm enough in there. Now, march into that bathroom and strip, or I'll really start forcing my help on you!"

It was simpler to obey. And as soon as she was standing under the blessedly warm spray of the shower, it hardly seemed to matter where she was, so long as this warmth continued to cascade over her. By the time she emerged, she felt more like herself again—not that terror-stricken, bedraggled creature who'd sobbed against the steering wheel in hysterical despair.

She discovered that her own pale green robe was hanging on the bathroom door and her filthy, dripping clothes had been removed from the floor, where she'd left them. Ethan must have quietly slipped in to perform these errands while she was oblivious to everything but the hot, soothing relief of the shower.

The sight of her robe reminded Jess of where she'd last seen it, lying on the toppled pile of debris she'd left behind in her mad, ill-fated flight from the cabin. It was because of this robe that she'd slipped and fallen, knocking over that table and awakening Ethan. How ludicrous it all started to seem, like something out of a slapstick comedy routine.

"All I needed was a clown suit," she thought, remembering her own undignified pratfall amid the clatter of falling objects. She was actually chuckling to herself as she stepped out of the bathroom, much to Ethan's surprise.

"You're looking better. Now, sit by the fire and drink this," he said, thrusting a mug of scalding-hot cocoa into her hands. He was wearing dry clothes now, and he'd toweled his hair dry in such a way that it stuck straight up from his head in funny little tufts that completely undid his usual look of effortless, rugged elegance. Jess felt a sudden, heart-tugging ache of love for him as she fought the urge to smooth down the absurd spikes of unruly dark hair.

"Aye, aye, sir!" she answered him cheekily, hiding her feelings under a show of playful defiance. She sat down on one of the chairs that had been drawn up near the fire, and was thankful that the floor pillows had been moved elsewhere.

"What were you laughing about just now, when you came in?" Ethan asked. His voice was so studiedly casual that Jess instinctively knew he hadn't wanted to ask that question but just couldn't restrain himself.

"Myself," she answered, smiling wryly. "The way I tiptoed around my cabin so cautiously, afraid to make a sound for fear of waking you up, and then, at the last minute, managed to bring half the stuff in the room crashing down around my head! The whole scene seems so ridiculous to me now—so pointless."

"Pointless?" he prompted eagerly.

"Because it didn't get me anywhere. I've wound up right back in the same spot I tried to run from."

"Not quite," he said moodily. "You're not in my arms." Jess felt her face go stiff, but before she could even try to speak, he said, "I'm sorry. I shouldn't have said that. I'm glad you can find something to laugh at. A sense of humor is a good sign that you've recovered from your bout with the cold." And then he forced a teasing note into his voice. "I guess there'll be no need after all for me to apply the age-old remedy for hypothermia."

"And what might that be?" Jess asked suspiciously. She was pretty sure she knew, but she wanted to encourage Ethan's sense of humor to start functioning again too. It made things easier.

"Skin-to-skin contact, preferably administered in the buff, with both parties wrapped up together in a dry sleeping bag."

"Very cozy. I'm sure it must prove highly effective," she replied. "But you're right. I'm completely recovered now, so it won't be necessary to put it to the test on my account."

"What about me?" he asked. "I think I feel an attack of the shivers coming on right this minute."

"Try drinking some of this cocoa. It's guaranteed to boil the lining right off your whole digestive tract."

"That reminds me!" he exclaimed, dashing over to the stove. "I've heated up a pan of soup. It's important to drink warm liquids."

"But I'm perfectly warm now, Ethan!" Jess protested gently. He ignored her. "What a bully you are!" she accused as he proceeded to dish up the soup and set it out with rolls and crackers on a small table in front of the fire. "I'm surprised you haven't tried to force brandy down my throat! But don't let me give you any ideas," she quickly added, "because I detest brandy."

"I wouldn't do that," he replied seriously, "because alcohol is the worst thing to take when you're cold. It may give an illusion of warmth, but it actually causes the body to lose heat faster because it dilates the blood vessels." He brought his own bowl of soup over to the fire, where he sat down opposite Jess.

"What a gold mine of information you are, Ethan! Everything I always wanted to know about hypothermia . . . and a lot more! Hypothermia in ten easy lessons!" Jess knew she was ranting, but she couldn't help it. She was starting to feel giddy from the strain between them, plus a delayed reaction to her watery adventures seemed to be setting in.

"Eat your soup," Ethan ordered gently, and the smile he gave her was so understanding that Jess wanted to cry. "There *is* something else we need to talk about," he went on. "I know you're ready to collapse, but we really should settle this tonight. I don't know how you plan to deal with this . . . situation between us, but I have a suggestion to offer."

Eight

"Now, wait a minute," Jess protested. "I won't let you get away with it this time."

"Get away with what?"

"I've finally caught on to your devious tricks, Ethan Jamieson! Every time you want to talk me into something that's to your advantage, you make darn sure the discussion takes place while we're *eating*. No wonder you're such a success in the food business— you know exactly how to exploit the joys of food for your own nefarious purposes!"

"Now I've heard everything."

"The facts speak for themselves!" she accused, warming to her subject. "It all started when you wormed your way into my cabin with that pint of ice cream, and in no time flat you were stalking me while you ate *my* chowder. Next you were plying me with croissants and cappuccino so you could bamboozle me into agreeing to drive you all up and down the coast. And ever since then you've been feeding me like a prize pig and wrapping me around your little pinkie the whole time." She shook her head in mock disgust. "When I think of the way you practically hypnotized me with that omelet of yours! And the way you used steak and salad to help seduce me tonight—"

"*Seduce* you! Now, just a minute—"

"And now you're trying to make me change my mind about leaving, even though you promised you wouldn't! You're hoping that soup and crackers will soften me up so you can convince me to stay."

"Right," he drawled sarcastically. "And I'm baiting my trap with soup out of a can and crackers that are definitely on the stale side. Of course. Such fine cuisine no woman could possibly resist! Honestly, Jess." He ended on a note of exasperated amusement, and his eyes invited her to admit the whole idea was preposterously funny.

"That just shows what a pushover you think I am," she accused in a shaky voice. "You think all you have to do is smile that damn smile of yours and I'll be right back in the palm of your hand." And it could still happen if she didn't keep fighting him for all she was worth. But suddenly she was very tired of struggling, and she had to keep blinking back the tears.

"Jess!" Ethan pleaded. "Stop it! You know that's not true! You're too tired and upset to think straight. So far you've only gotten one thing right—I *am* hoping to convince you to stay in Mendocino till the end of your vacation."

"I knew it!"

He went on as if she hadn't spoken. "My suggestion is that you stay here and let *me* be the one to leave."

"What?" She lifted incredulous, tear-filled green eyes to stare at him.

"I haven't forgotten that you came here to paint, Jess," he said gently. "As you've pointed out several times, this is a *working* holiday for you. Well, won't it rather disrupt your work if you pack up and leave now? If one of us has to go, I should be the one."

"That's . . . that's very generous of you," Jess said, while her mind whirled in confusion. Once again he'd caught her off guard. It wasn't fair that he should be so understanding just when she was trying so hard to fall out of love with him!

"Then, you agree?" he asked.

She gave a small, uncertain laugh. "I'd be crazy not to, wouldn't I? That is"—she hesitated—"if you're sure that you're willing."

"The only thing I'm sure of is that it'll hurt like hell to say good-bye," he answered harshly. "So please don't ask me to be *willing,* Jess! Let's just say I'll do it." He paused, and then added quietly, "On one condition."

"I might have guessed. What?"

"Before I disappear out of your life, don't you think I have the right to know *why*?" Though he tried to speak calmly, the violence of his emotions gnawed away at the level surface of his words. "I thought we had everything going for us, Jess. I thought we'd be spending the rest of our lives together. Tonight, when we made love, I could have sworn that you loved me, and even after all that's happened, I'm still not convinced that you don't! So what went wrong? Why did you run away? I have to know."

Jess stared at him, shocked by the agony she read in his face. This was the man she loved, and he was hurting like this because of her. And as she tried to think how she could explain her actions to him, she was attacked by a sudden new swarm of doubts. Her decision to run away had been made in a moment of weak, blind panic—had it really been the *right* decision?

She had run because she feared she couldn't preserve her identity as an artist if she fell more deeply under Ethan's sensual spell. But maybe she'd been unfair to both of them. After all tonight Ethan had shown how understanding and supportive he could be in time of need. And Jess wondered if she herself weren't stronger than she'd given herself credit for in those first startled moments of panic and despair. Maybe she *could* hold her own in a relationship with Ethan. Didn't they deserve a chance to try to make it work? But what if she ended up being swallowed alive by love, losing her work and her sense of who she was? How could she take such a risk? Her thoughts went round and round and got exactly nowhere.

"Dammit, Jess! All I'm asking for is an explanation!" Ethan burst out impatiently, startling Jess out of her troubled thoughts. "Just please tell me what it is about me that brings that scared look to your eyes." He took a deep, ragged breath. "Tell me, and then I promise I'll leave first thing in the morning."

His words sounded in her ears like the slam of a closing door. "Of course you're entitled to an explanation," she told him, slumping back in her chair with a weary sigh. "But it's not going to be easy . . . for either of us. We've both been through too much already tonight, and I don't know if I can take any more." It was true. Her nerves had been stretched to the breaking point, and now she felt utterly drained. "Couldn't you give me a rain check? Say . . . twenty-four hours?"

"Perhaps it would be best to wait. I just assumed you'd want to get rid of me as soon as possible," he said with grim humor. "You do understand that I won't leave Mendocino until I've heard your explanation." Jess nodded. "And if you pull another stunt like running off in the middle of the night, all bets are off, so be warned!"

"I won't try that again, I promise. There's no need. You've given me your word, and I trust you . . . now."

"Thanks. Just don't trust me too far," he said in a gravelly voice. "I'm not made of steel." And on that cryptic note, he stood up and began clearing away the half-eaten bowls of soup. It was time to say good night.

Only after Jess was out the door did it occur to her that she hadn't thanked him for saving her life tonight. *If* indeed her life had been in any danger. She still wasn't sure about that. Or about anything at all except her body's need to collapse into bed.

Neither the weight of the decision she had to make nor the chill of the bed sheets could keep sleep from swooping over her like a black velvet curtain, obliterating the dizzy circling of her thoughts.

The morning brought lots of sunshine and bright blue sky, but no answers. Jess decided she needed to get away somewhere by herself to think things through. Somewhere where she couldn't hear the rattle of Ethan's breakfast dishes or his muffled curse when he burned the toast. At least she didn't have to worry that her behavior had interfered with Ethan's appetite, she reflected wryly as she stared at her own untouched dish of cereal.

But that was small consolation when he knocked on her door a few minutes later and she got a good look at his face. He might still be eating, but he obviously hadn't slept much last night. And he hadn't shaved this morning.

"Got a minute?" he asked abruptly. "I need to talk to you."

"But . . . it's too soon!" she protested in dismay. "I need more time."

"It's not about *us*," he added quickly. "It's about your paintings."

"My paintings?" Jess echoed in astonishment.

"Yes. I'd like to use some of them in the opening exhibit of Fiori's new Wine Gallery. And before you say something nasty about how you wouldn't be caught dead with your paintings on display in a grocery store, just listen to me."

Jess's jaw had dropped at his first request, but now she snapped it shut to hold back the emphatic denial she was just about to utter. The least she could do was listen.

"You've got the wrong idea about this gallery," he started off by saying. "It's not going to be some trite assortment of reproductions and mass-produced 'originals.' Fiori's has a reputation for excellence, and we're not about to undermine our good name by launching a second-rate art gallery. We've hired professional artistic consultants and we intend to display only top-quality work."

"Perhaps I was too quick to judge," Jess admitted hesitantly. "I'm sorry." Her prejudice against the Wine Gallery idea had been basically irrational, she realized. There was no reason it couldn't turn out to be a fine addition to the San Francisco art community. But why was Ethan suddenly so interested in her paintings?

"Think about it, Jess," he said, and his gaze was direct and compelling. "This could be a real opportunity for your talent to get the recognition it deserves."

Suddenly Jess felt a hard knot of suspicion tighten in her chest. "What's behind this offer of yours?"

It took Ethan a second to realize what she was implying.

"How dare you cheapen everything we've shared by asking such a question! I think your paintings are right for my gallery. Period. No strings attached. My offer has nothing to do with our personal relationship."

"Then, I apologize," Jess said, swallowing. "But it just wouldn't be right for me to accept that kind of favor from you under the circumstances."

"Dammit, Jess! That's nonsense!"

"Can't you see that the whole situation is impossible?" she pleaded. "I appreciate your offer, but my answer has to be no." And she shut the door in his disbelieving face so she wouldn't be tempted to reach out and grab this glittering opportunity regardless of whether it was right or wrong.

Because she knew it was wrong. There was no way Ethan could be objective about her paintings, and just because he liked them was not reason enough for her work to get into Fiori's gallery. He'd hired professional consultants to make those decisions, and the last thing he should be doing was going behind their backs to promise Jess a place in the exhibit. *They* were the experts, not Ethan. And she would be the worst kind of opportunist if she tried to advance her career by exploiting their relationship in that way.

Twenty minutes later Jess succeeded in extricating Old Betsy from the muddy parking lot, and then set off in search of broad, empty vistas of sea and sky, hoping that her thoughts might become as clear as the windswept scenery. But she might as well have stayed in the parking lot, because her thoughts were about as clear as the mud there.

She spent the first part of the day trying to find the inner courage to face the challenge of a relationship that might end up as a constant struggle for emotional survival. But every time she thought she'd reached a decision, all the old fears rushed in and doused that newborn spark of confidence. How could she possibly dare to take such a risk?

So she spent the next hour trying to resign herself to giving Ethan up forever. But she found herself picturing the laughter and understanding in his tawny eyes, the quick, graceful strength of his hands, and the bone-melting warmth of his long, slow smile. Even now her mouth was hungering for the sweet fire of his kisses. And those were just the external things. What about the caring, thoughtful, challenging depths of the man she loved? What about his need for her?

So she tried to forget the whole dilemma and concentrate on her painting for a while. But she couldn't. Couldn't forget. Couldn't concentrate. And, worst of all, couldn't paint. Grimly she forced herself to at least make some rough sketches, but the result was a lifeless parody of her usual work. It was as if some vital force within her were blocked.

At last she gave up in disgust and sat hunched over her sketch pad, wanting to cry out with frustration and despair. She *had* to find an answer soon—it wasn't fair to keep Ethan dangling like this. And she couldn't stand too much more of it herself. There must be some possibility she had overlooked, some key factor that would tell her what to do.

By the time she got back to the cabin, Jess knew if she didn't make her mind up soon she was going to lose it completely. She was so tense and on edge that the sound of a chair scraping against the floor in the next room sent her jumping a foot in the air.

She held her breath for several agonizing seconds as heavy footsteps pounded on the linoleum next door. When she heard Ethan's door slam she actually bit down hard on her lower lip. Her twenty-four hours weren't up already, were they? But then, as the footsteps faded away in the other direction, she wiped her sweaty palms on her jeans and sank into a chair. Another reprieve.

But for how long? Her chest ached and her muscles were tight as steel wires as she sat waiting, straining her ears to catch any small sound that might mean Ethan was returning. She sat like that for five minutes, and then she decided to take action.

She hadn't used her portable tape recorder since she'd first arrived. Once she'd caught her first glimpse of the Mendocino coast, she hadn't wanted any recorded, man-made music to intrude on the natural peace and beauty of the place. She'd loved the feeling of being in another world, cut off from the sights and sounds of her busy existence in the city. Until now, the sound of waves and sea gulls had been music enough for Jess, and she'd forgotten she even had the tape recorder along. But this was an emergency.

With all the trembling, desperate urgency of a sick person measuring out a dose of medicine that promised instant relief, Jess plugged in the tape recorder, inserted a cassette, and adjusted the headphones over her ears. With one push of a button, music filled her ears, blotting out all the little sounds that had been tearing so savagely at her ravaged nerves.

Jess gave a nervous trill of ironic laughter as she recognized the early Beatles tune on the tape— "Help!" How fitting, she thought. If only she *could* turn to someone for help in sorting out this puzzle. If there were just someone she could talk to. But there was no one. It was hard to make close friends in a big city when you worked at a series of temporary jobs and spent all your free time painting. In fact, it suddenly occurred to Jess that her closest friend was a man she had met only a few days ago. A man named Ethan Jamieson. And he was the last person she could ask for help now. Or was he?

The thought was so unexpected that it left her stunned. And then she began to wonder why it hadn't occurred to her sooner. Why had she struggled alone with this problem for so long, when the obvious person to tell her what she needed to know was right in the next room? Ethan *knew himself* as few people knew themselves. He had a clear view of his own strengths and weaknesses. Time and again Jess had been surprised by how perceptive he was when it came to understanding the human heart and mind. And he was a truthful man. So . . . Ethan himself could tell her what to expect in their relationship. If he told her that the artist within her had nothing to fear from loving him, she could believe him.

Until now, she had treated Ethan as an adversary. Her experience with Cliff had frightened her so deeply that she hadn't been ready to accept any man as a friend. But it was time to put the past behind her. And it was long past time to talk openly and honestly with Ethan, to share with him her doubts and fears, and to hear from his own lips whether he thought they could work together to resolve their differences.

Jess felt each taut muscle in her body gradually release its burden of tension. The future was still uncertain, but she suddenly felt very hopeful that she and Ethan could sort it out together. She leaned back against the couch, at peace with herself once more. Her limbs started to feel heavy and relaxed, and the music from the headphones sounded blurred and indistinct. Slowly she closed her eyes. . . .

Something startled her, and she opened her lids on to blackness. Briefly she panicked, adrift on a sea of silent darkness, with no memory of how she came to be there. Seconds later she remembered that she'd been listening to music, and realized that she must have fallen asleep. But why were the lights out, and why wasn't her tape player making at least a faint mechanical hum? Her brain was still numb with sleep, so it was another few seconds before it occurred to her that a fuse must have blown.

Impatiently she yanked the headphones off her ears, and suddenly became aware of a loud, urgent knocking at the door. When she jumped up and opened it, Ethan's dark silhouette was outlined against the starlit sky.

"Thank God you're here!" he exclaimed. "I was beginning to think you'd gone out walking and wandered off a cliff into the ocean! Do you realize you haven't made a sound for over two hours? And I had to pound on this door for five minutes before you answered."

"I was asleep," Jess said groggily. "What time is it, anyway?"

"Only a little before ten. Sorry I woke you, but I didn't expect you to be sleeping this early. Now that you're up, may I borrow your flashlight?"

"Why?"

"Because we've blown another fuse, in case you hadn't noticed. And I can't find my matches."

"Oh." It wasn't like him to be unprepared in an emergency.

"And because I was worried about you!" he confessed impatiently. "I saw your car in the lot, but I couldn't detect any signs of life coming through the wall. I had to make sure you were okay."

"I'm fine." Jess looked at him uncertainly. His eyes weren't quite meeting hers.

"All right, then, I admit it!" he exploded, as if answering an accusation. "The real reason I came was because I couldn't keep away from you anymore! Even if I'd known you were perfectly safe, even if the fuse hadn't blown, I'd still have found an excuse to see you. I can't take another night of it, Jess!"

Suddenly the darkness was alive with powerful emotions that seemed to crackle in the air between them like the rattling of a hidden snake. Jess couldn't see Ethan's face, but she heard the desperation in his voice, and it caused her to take a step back in surprise. She was so used to thinking of him as a man in control of his own emotions—patient, reasonable, and understanding. But now she was suddenly reminded of the man who'd turned on her like a wounded beast of prey that very first night.

"Another night of *what*?" she asked shakily.

"Of wanting you so much I have to spend every hour fighting the urge to break down your door and make love to you. Of wanting so terribly to convince you we belong together that I'm tempted to use physical force. It's no use pretending I can fight it much longer—not when you're so close I can hear you turn over in bed at night."

Jess backed another step away from him.

"I'm begging you to keep your promise to give me an explanation. Please, give it to me now, tonight, and let me leave here before I do something we'll both regret. It's the only way, Jess."

"You're right. We do need to talk tonight," she said, making her voice matter-of-fact in an attempt to calm him. "Why don't I get you that flashlight first?" Groping her way across the darkened room, she asked casually, as if no emotional conflagration were imminent, "What blew the fuse this time? Got any ideas?"

There was an awkward silence, and Jess was afraid Ethan would refuse to let the conversation drop back to such a mundane topic. He had worked himself up to the boiling point, and he was ripe for confrontation. When he finally answered, she gave a secret sigh of relief.

"I'm not sure what blew the fuse. I was using the toaster, but that's never been a problem before. Maybe it was responding to telekinetic powers I didn't even know I had. To give me an excuse to come knocking at your door, you see."

"That's an interesting theory." She chuckled. "But I think it had more to do with the fact that I had my tape player on at the same time, and I guess the wiring just couldn't handle that together with the lights and the refrigerators *and* your toaster. So it's my fault. Sorry for the inconvenience. Here's the flashlight." She flicked it on and turned around.

Ethan stood absolutely still as the pale gleam of the flashlight suddenly revealed her to him. His eyes drank in the sensuous shadowed curves of her face, the luminous silvery green of her eyes, and the glimmering waves of her hair flowing down to her breasts. His gaze lingered there, savoring the rounded flesh that lay beneath the pale green robe. She looked fragile as a lily, but the look was deceiving, for he had known the sweet, glorious strength of her body as she arched against him in the act of love. The thought of it now made him tremble, and his hands yearned to untie the knotted sash at her waist and touch the hot-blooded woman. He could almost taste her on his lips.

He shut his eyes, but her image still burned in his brain, and he found himself taking a step toward her. Abruptly he turned away, clenching his fists.

"Toss me the flashlight," he said. Without a word Jess obeyed, watching its beam arc wildly through the air before it came to rest in Ethan's quick, sure grasp. And then he was gone.

But she knew he would be back. He wanted her explanation tonight. And he wanted to make love to her. Jess had seen the look on his face, and she knew how close he had come to losing control. She wanted to make sure that didn't occur, so she shoved a heavy chest of drawers across the door. Soon the lights came on, and her heart began to beat faster, and then it beat faster still when she heard Ethan's footsteps approaching. He knocked.

"I'm leaving your flashlight here by the door," he called. "Thanks for lending it to me." He looked startled when Jess immediately opened the door about a foot's width, and she in turn was surprised to see that he was already turning to walk away.

"How did you manage to change the fuse so fast?" she asked. "I thought we were all out of replacements."

"We were. I swiped an extra one from another cabin." He looked at her and took a deep breath. "Jess, I . . . I've changed my mind. Our talk is going to have to wait till daylight and take place in a more public spot. I'm just not feeling too trustworthy tonight." His smile was a crooked, wavering line that made Jess ache inside.

"There's no need to wait," she insisted. "We can talk now, like this, with the door between us."

"You don't understand, Jess. The way I feel right now, that door doesn't mean very much. I'll see you tomorrow." He started to move away.

"Ethan! Wait!" Jess pleaded, unable to bear the thought of this hanging over their heads for another night. Through the narrow opening, she watched him slowly turn around. Something in his taut, wary stance warned her that she was playing with fire, but the solid barrier of the wooden chest against the door gave her courage. "We've *got* to talk. Don't worry about the door. I've got something heavy shoved across it," she confessed, unprepared for the anger that suddenly flared in his white, set face.

"So that's what you think of me. You've got even less faith in me than I have in myself," he said bitterly. "Well, I can't say I blame you, but I don't think a discussion that has to take place on opposite sides of a barred door has very much to offer. Let's just skip it, okay?" He turned on his heel and left her.

"Ethan!" she screamed, tugging at the barricade she had erected. All she could think of was her need to bring him back, make him listen. "Don't you see, it's not *you* I don't trust. It's myself!" Still he continued walking away from her. "Please come back and give me a chance to explain," she desperately begged his retreating back.

But suddenly it wasn't retreating anymore, and

then it wasn't his back, either—it was Ethan himself, looming in the doorway with an expression on his face that shook Jess right down to the soles of her bare feet.

"What the hell are you trying to do to me?" he demanded hoarsely.

His face was only inches away from hers, and his eyes blazed so fiercely they seemed to sear the skin on Jess's cheeks as she met his gaze. She felt gripped by a wild surge of emotion, so powerful that it blocked her throat like a giant hand clamped across her windpipe. She couldn't answer him.

"Don't play games with me!" he rasped. "I've been doing my damnedest to keep my promise to you, Jess. But I'm beginning to wonder if that's what you really want! Why did you call me back? Have you changed your mind about me? Is that what this is all about?"

"I'm not sure yet," she whispered guiltily, afraid to look at him. "I just don't know! I'm so confused. But I need to talk to you. I want to explain why I've been afraid of loving you. I called you back because I want to talk about it now, tonight."

"Please wait till tomorrow," he said, and his voice held a kind of desperate gentleness. "*Please.* Tonight is too dangerous. Especially if you're confused. I want you to be *sure*, Jess."

"But what's so risky about just talking? We've got a very solid chest of drawers blocking the door between us. What could happen?" And she gave a nervous little trill of laughter. That was a mistake, as she knew when Ethan flushed with sudden fury.

"Since you find it so damn amusing, maybe I should *show* you what could happen! *This.*"

He moved so swiftly she didn't have time to draw back. And she wasn't sure she wanted to, as all her senses leaped in tumultuous response to his touch. There was just enough space between the door and its frame for a man's forearm to reach through, but that was all it took. Ethan's fingers thrust like lightning into that opening and snatched at the belt of

Jess's robe. With one quick tug he had her body arched against the narrow crack, while his foot and knee held the door to keep it from shutting under her helpless weight.

Still holding her by the knotted cord round her waist, he slid the fingers of his other hand through the doorway to softly entangle themselves in the silken masses of her hair. Jess shivered with excitement as his knuckles brushed against her skin, and then she felt herself submitting to the gentle but inexorable pressure of his fingers on her neck as he drew her face close to his in the narrow space between the door and doorjamb.

"No, Ethan," she tried to protest. "We need to talk first." But then she forgot everything but her need of him as her lips parted under the fierce hunger of his kiss.

His mouth tasted hers with starved abandon, and Jess moaned deep in her throat as their tongues lunged together like frenzied lovers. She felt his fingers move slowly down the curve of her neck and then straight down to the cleft between her breasts, and she turned her body into the narrow opening of the door so that one firm breast and taut nipple were pressed against his hand. She heard his sharp intake of breath, and the sound sent new sparks of arousal flickering through her.

Now he was struggling to untie the sash of her robe, and Jess shared his breathless urgency. She wanted more of his touch, and she didn't care where it led her. When the folds of her robe fell away to reveal the heated, yearning flesh beneath, Ethan bent his head to take her breast into his mouth. Jess gasped as the tug of his lips and flick of his tongue sent her whole body tumbling headlong into the vortex of passion.

He lowered his mouth along her flesh, first lapping with his tongue against her belly and then licking a trail of unbearable delight along the smooth flesh of her inner thigh. When his tongue had traveled to her knee, he began the journey up her body again, only this time he caressed her with only a warm breath that he blew out through softly pursed lips. Jess had never experienced anything so teasingly sensuous as that intimate current of air playing along her thighs, rippling in the hair that curled between her legs, awakening a thousand tiny sensations that all added up to one overwhelming urge.

She uttered small strangled cries without being aware that they came from her own throat, and Ethan took her lips again with a kiss that throbbed and beat in her mouth like the fevered pulsing of her own heart.

"Let me in, Jess. Let me in," he whispered, as his tongue ravished the delicate contours of her ear and his fingers danced lightly between her legs.

"Help me push this out of the way," she gasped, pulling at the old wooden chest of drawers that was her last barrier against him. He released her for mere seconds as his shoulder shoved against the door, forcing the heavy piece of furniture back far enough so he could step into the room.

He shut the door behind him and picked her up by the waist. Swiftly he carried her to the bed, and Jess clung to him as he lowered her onto it. Propping himself up with one hand on the mattress, he bent over her for a searing, shattering kiss, while with his other hand he unbuckled his jeans. Jess's hands joined his as she tugged his pants down to his knees, but when he would have undressed completely, she cried out in frantic need and wrapped her legs around him, forcing his hard body against hers.

"Now, please, now!" she whispered, and he answered with a shuddering thrust that turned her body to a rippling mass of breathless pleasure. Twisting and turning, arching and plunging, they rode each other like storm-driven waves crashing and thundering against the shore. At last Jess felt herself lifted in a great dizzying spiral that dissolved her mind and body into shining, weightless flecks of sea foam and flung her, gasping, onto the soft, tranquil sands of the shore. Ethan clung to her like a drowning man as the pounding force of the surf within claimed him also for the final leap and plummet to earth.

When it was over, Jess lay still and let her thoughts come trickling back to her. Everything seemed so simple now. There had been no need for talking after all. This thing between them was as inevitable as the ocean tides. This was the very force of life itself that she had tried to deny and hold back. How foolish she had been. She still didn't know what her relationship with Ethan would bring, and there were still many things that needed to be said between them, but the real decision had been made. You couldn't run away from the very essence of life.

She turned her head to look at him. He lay face downward beside her, and something in his stillness suddenly frightened her. She reached out to stroke his rumpled dark hair, and her hand paused as she felt the tensed muscles of his neck.

"Ethan, what's wrong?" she whispered, laying her cheek against his shoulder.

"How can you even ask me that?" he asked in a low, choked voice. Abruptly he turned to face her, and his mouth was twisted with bitterness. Suddenly Jess knew things weren't going to be so simple after all.

Nine

"I broke my promise." He said the words angrily, but his eyes were dark with pain, and Jess had to resist the urge to hug him soothingly to her breast.

"It desn't matter, Ethan. I was just as much to blame as you were."

"It does matter! You told me you were confused, and then I went right ahead and took advantage of your confusion. That's exactly what I promised *not* to do."

"But Ethan, how can you regret what happened? Maybe it started wrong, but it ended up *right*. And I don't feel confused anymore."

"That doesn't give me back my self-respect, Jess. I've always thought of myself as someone whose word could be trusted. Now I find that's not true. I have to face the fact that I wasn't strong enough to live up to my principles, and it hurts."

"And you're angry with me because of it, aren't you?" Jess exclaimed with sudden insight. "You resent the fact that you lost control of yourself over *me*."

"You're right," he admitted after a short, tense silence. "Even though I take full responsibility for my own actions, I can't help feeling that you secretly *wanted* me to break down and behave the way I did. And that makes me feel . . . manipulated." His eyes met hers in a dark look of accusation and misery, and Jess felt her heart sink.

"That's not fair, Ethan," she murmured. "We both know how much I've wanted you physically all along, but I had no intention of letting this happen the way it did. I wasn't playing games, believe me. I was just determined to talk things over with you so I could decide what to do. And then the whole situation got out of hand. I'm just sorry I didn't know my own mind a lot sooner, because it would have made things easier for both of us. I guess I was just too frightened to be sure of anything."

"What was there to be frightened of?" Ethan burst out impatiently. "I've tried and tried during these past days to come up with some reason for this fear you have of me, but nothing makes sense! Dammit, Jess, it's time you told me what's going on!"

"Yes, it's time." But she wished he were in a more understanding and forgiving mood. This explanation would have been difficult enough at the best of times, but right now seemed like a very bad time indeed. There was no way she could put it off any longer, however. She took a deep breath.

"Wait. Let's get dressed first," Ethan said abruptly. Jess didn't argue, though she would have preferred to stay as they were, lying close together on the bed where they'd just made love. She found it reassuring to be surrounded by the inescapable evidence of their recent act of total intimacy. Surely no misunderstanding could endure for long when Ethan was only a touch away. But he obviously wanted no reminders of what had taken place between them, since he regretted his part in it.

When they were dressed, Jess made coffee, and they sat at the table drinking it while she searched for the right words with which to begin.

"You won't understand my reactions to you unless you know about Cliff," she said. "I met him while working on a six-week temporary assignment last year at a large corporate office where he was a very up-and-coming executive. I was flattered that such a dynamic, handsome, successful man would be interested in me, but I didn't think he could be serious about me, so I kept my head. Until one day he asked me to marry him."

"And then you lost your head?"

"Yes. Cliff really had a talent for impressing people, including me. In my imagination I immediately endowed him with every good quality I'd ever looked for in a man, and then I proceeded to fall madly in love with the perfect image I'd just invented. I accepted his proposal, and we were engaged. Of course I realized that many of Cliff's goals and values in life were understandably different from those of a struggling artist like myself, but I thought he was so wonderful and our love was so perfect that nothing like that would ever matter."

"But it did?"

"Yes. After the early romantic glow faded a little, I began to discover things I didn't like about the man I thought I was so much in love with. The worst part was learning he had no respect for my work. To him, it seemed ludicrous that a grown woman would waste her time painting pictures when she didn't make money at it. Especially when it would have enhanced the social prestige of her fiancé so much more if she'd pursued a more lucrative profession." Jess paused and took a deep breath.

"I was hurt by his attitude," she continued, "but I thought we could work it out. I explained how I felt, hoping he'd try to be more understanding. Instead he took it as a personal insult that I wasn't willing to give up my messy, inconvenient little 'hobby' to please him. It got so we quarreled about it every time we were together, and he retaliated for my 'stubbornness' by putting me down every chance he got. He told me I was not only lousy as an artist, but also lousy in bed and a total failure as a woman."

"My God, Jess! Why did you put up with it?"

"Because I thought I was in love with him. And I had this crazy hope that if I could just make him see how vitally important painting was to me, he'd *understand* and then everything would be perfect again."

"It sounds to me as if he knew all along how much it meant to you!" Ethan exclaimed. "That's exactly what he couldn't forgive. He wanted to take away the part of you that was independent of him, so that he'd feel in absolute control. Not exactly a healthy attitude."

"No. I realized that later. He had a sick obsession with trying to dominate and manipulate people. I can't think why he picked someone like me to get engaged to in the first place!"

"Probably because you were a challenge. So what made you finally come to your senses and get rid of this guy?"

"How do you know it was *my* decision?"

"I just know. I can't see you letting anyone drown that creative, independent spark of yours without one hell of a fight. And sooner or later you'd realize this Cliff fellow wasn't worth all the struggle. Now, tell me, what happened?"

This was the hard part. She had never told anyone about that final confrontation with Cliff. But now she must tell Ethan, and she must try to tell him calmly. "One night when we were at my apartment, Cliff started making his usual demands that I quit 'pretending' to be an artist and concentrate on being his fiancée. I was pretty fed up by then, so I didn't even try to make a respectful plea for his understanding, the way I usually did. Instead, I yelled at him that I thought I could handle both roles just fine if he'd only stop being so selfish and small-minded about the whole thing."

"Bravo!" But Ethan's cheer went unnoticed by Jess, who was painfully reliving the traumatic events of that night.

"Cliff didn't say anything after that—he just stared out the window for a while. And then he grabbed me. I sensed the anger in him, but when he started to make love to me I managed to convince myself that it was just his way of trying to make up after our quarrel. So I went along with it. Until suddenly I realized that everything he was doing was meant as punishment. I could see it in his eyes and feel it in his touch. He wanted to control me. *That* was what gave him pleasure—the idea that he had sexual power over me. He started whispering in my ear how he was going to possess me over and over again until he had made me swear never to paint again. Only, he put it much more crudely than that."

Jess stopped, shaken by the wave of nausea that swept her even now at the memory. "When I saw what he was trying to do, I felt physically sick. I mean that literally. I told him I was going to throw up if he didn't leave, and he must have seen by the look on my face that I wasn't bluffing. Anyway, he left." She tried to laugh, but it hadn't seemed funny at the time and it didn't seem humorous to her now.

"I never wanted to see him again. He had tried to manipulate me sexually. He had exploited and debased what should have been an expression of love and desire between us, by turning it into a tool of violence and domination. And it finally hit me that he couldn't really have loved me if he was so determined to change me against my will. When I sent back his ring, all I felt was relief that it was finally over. Or so I thought."

She looked across the table at Ethan. His face was pale and his jaw was clenched so hard, the muscles twitched in his cheeks. It must be painful for him to hear the humiliating details of her relationship with another man. It wasn't exactly pleasant for Jess herself, having to expose her own weakness and stupidity over a man who was worth less than the hair on Ethan's knuckles.

"What else, Jess? What did that bastard do to you?"

"Nothing like what you're thinking," she said quickly. "He never touched me again. But . . . after I returned his ring, he returned something that I'd given *him*. A painting." Her voice wobbled out of control, and she fought to keep it firm. "I'd given it to him early in our relationship, before I found out how much he despised art. To me, it was the most precious gift I could have given, because that painting was the best piece of work I've ever done. *Was*."

"Oh, my God!" Ethan whispered in horror. "Are you going to tell me that he . . . defaced your painting? Was that the way he gave it back to you?"

"Yes." The answer felt wrenched from her throat. "I won't even tell you what he did to it—it was unspeakable. And I felt as if *I* had been violated and defiled. Can you understand that?"

"I think so." His eyes were full of troubled empathy. "It was your work, your vision of life, your creation that he mutilated. It was a piece of yourself. He was telling you what he would have liked to do to *you*." Ethan reached across the table and took her hand in a warm, comforting grip. "Did you ever consider that you might have been *lucky* he had that painting to vent his viciousness on? What he did was a symbolic form of rape—it could have been the real thing."

Jess shuddered. "You must think I was an utter fool to get involved with a man like that in the first place. But I had no way of knowing what he was really like until I was already in pretty deep."

"I know you're not a fool," Ethan reassured her. "We all make mistakes in judging other people, especially when they pretend to be something they're not. But you can't let one emotionally sick individual turn you against all the men in the world. We're not all like him."

"I know that. But after Cliff, I swore I'd avoid that type of man like the plague. I decided the next man I fell in love with would have to be an artist, or at least someone in a creative profession—someone who would share my interests and values. *Not* the business-executive type. *Not* the three-piece-suit type. And then you came along." She gave a wry smile.

"And you see *me* as the three-piece-suit type?" Ethan gave a bark of incredulous laughter, but the merriment in his face was quickly subdued beneath a troubled frown. "There's something here I don't understand," he said. "I realize I don't quite fit this image you have of your perfect mate, since I can't claim to be an artist. But surely *that* can't be what's keeping us apart! You wouldn't let something so silly stand in the way of what we could have together!"

"It wasn't silly! Haven't you heard a thing I've been saying? I've had one disastrous experience with a money-obsessed man who was contemptuous of my work. I couldn't handle another."

Suddenly the room was so still that Jess could hear the wind rustling in the grass outside. Ethan's eyes were like two slits in a fortified wall of steel. His hand clenched on hers and then slowly pulled away.

"Let me get this straight," he said. His voice was colder and harder than Jess had ever heard it before. "You're actually comparing *me* to that psychopath you were engaged to? You think I'm like *that*?"

"Of course not, but there were some similarities . . ."

"Such as *what*? When have I tried to manipulate you, sexually or otherwise? I've let *you* call the shots! You say I'm obsessed with money, yet the only time I remember the subject's even coming up was when Beryl accused me of not spending enough of it on her. And as for leveling a charge against me of having a 'contemptuous' attitude about your work, that's pure hogwash! My offer to include your paintings in Fiori's opening exhibit should be proof enough of *that*. It's obvious you don't have the faintest notion what I really think about your paintings."

"Oh, yes, I do! Until today, the first and last thing you wanted to know about them was how much they *cost*. As for your gallery offer—that just shows that you're willing to use my paintings as business tools to help you make money selling wine. And if that isn't a good indication of a crassly commercial attitude, I don't know what is!"

"Did it never occur to you that I might have asked

about the price of your paintings in the first place because I liked them so much I was seriously interested in *buying* them? You never gave me a chance to express an aesthetic opinion of your work—you started right off by telling me you weren't interested in anything I had to say on the subject."

Jess vaguely remembered that she *had* said something of the kind, that first evening.

"And as for your opinion of my Wine Gallery idea, what gives you the right to condemn my motives and attitudes, when you have no idea what they really are? What's so crassly commercial about caring enough to create a beautiful, tasteful atmosphere in which people can shop for wine? What's so morally wrong about giving artists an opportunity to show their work in a gallery where it'll be seen by scores of people every day?"

His words began to hit home. Why *had* she jumped to such conclusions about him? Why had she been so quick to condemn? In the face of Ethan's furious rebuttal, she found it difficult to recall all the little fragments of evidence that had seemed to add up to such a damning case against him. What stood out in her memory now was the way he had made her *feel*.

"Maybe it was illogical, but I still felt *overwhelmed* by you, Ethan! Sexually and emotionally. And it frightened me. Have you forgotten our first encounter? I haven't. You forced me to submit to your kisses and your groping hands, as an expression of your anger and contempt. I know that's not your usual behavior, and I'm sure you regret having done it, but it just wasn't a reassuring first impression! It was too much like Cliff. And even after you apologized, you still came on so strong. I was afraid of being overpowered by it all."

"I can't blame you for that," Ethan conceded, grimacing. "But what about later? I gave you time. I waited till you were ready, and you *were* ready, Jess! I thought you knew me by then. You knew I loved you. So how could you possibly believe I would treat you the way Cliff did?"

"But I only knew one side of you, Ethan—the tolerant, easygoing side. The man who chose to spend his vacation at a remote, rustic place like Bill's Cabins. It was the other side of you I was afraid of—the magnate who would measure value and success in monetary terms. I was afraid that my work and my commitment to it would have no value in your eyes, since I'm not financially successful at it. I was afraid your attitude would be patronizing and hostile, like Cliff's."

"So now we're back to this mythical attitude of mine! If you'd ever once bothered to ask, I would have been happy to tell you my views—which, incidentally, bear no resemblance to the ones you've attributed to me. But it seems you preferred to try me and convict me on the basis of your own prejudice against successful businessmen in three-piece suits. That's what it boils down to, Jess!"

"But Ethan—"

"Right from the first, you had me pegged as some sort of bullying Neanderthal with dollar signs in my eyes. And if all the time we've spent together hasn't changed your mind, then nothing I could say *now* is going to convince you. So there's no point in talking." He thrust himself to his feet and stood towering over her. "Good night, Jess."

"Ethan, wait! You don't understand—"

"No, Jess. *You* don't understand," he said with quiet vehemence. "I'm fed up to *here* with waiting for you really to see me." And he was gone before Jess could think how to stop him.

When the door closed behind him, Jess sat numb with shock and misery. She wanted to go after him and explain that she'd loved him in spite of all her doubts, and that tonight she'd finally committed herself to him. But she was paralyzed by the force of his hostility. He had said he was fed up with her and Jess was afraid he meant it. She certainly didn't blame him.

She'd misjudged him from the very beginning, and now that she realized how unjust her prejudice had been, it might be too late. She owed him an apology, but she feared Ethan wasn't willing to hear it. Perhaps he didn't even care anymore.

But she had to hope. Maybe by morning he'd be willing to listen to her and give her another chance. She had to believe that, or she'd never get through the dark hours until dawn. It took a long time to get to sleep, since her brain insisted on rehearsing over and over again what she would say to Ethan in the morning. And occasionally she was seized by a dreadful certainty that she'd lost him for good, and then she was powerless to stop the tears that soaked her pillow.

It was the sun shining against her closed eyelids that woke her the next morning. For an instant she felt only pleasure in its warm, golden touch on her face, but then she remembered. And she lay very still, wishing with all her might that she could hear Ethan's tuneful whistle from next door, or smell the appetizing aroma of a cooking omelet. But this morning wasn't going to be like that. Last night's quarrel wasn't the sort you could make up just by feeding somebody breakfast.

Reluctantly Jess opened her eyes. And sat up with a start as she realized that it must be very late if the sun was reaching this far into the room. How could she have overslept *this* morning, when it was so important that she see Ethan right away?

Hastily she washed and dressed, doing her best to camouflage the puffiness around her eyes that gave clear evidence of her tears the night before. Her hands shook with nervousness. Just as she was debating whether to delay a little longer by fortifying herself with coffee before facing Ethan, she heard a sound from next door.

Perhaps he was getting ready to go out. Without giving herself time to think better of it, she charged out the door, intent on saying her piece before he left. His door stood ajar, and she took this as another sign that he was on the point of departure. Her heart pounded as she lifted her hand to knock softly.

There was no answer. Jess pushed the door farther open and looked in. The room was clean and cold and empty. The bed had been stripped and the fireplace had been raked bare of ashes. A sharp, painful jab of fear slipped its way under Jess's ribs. Was she too late? Had Ethan so completely washed his hands of her that he'd left Mendocino without saying good-bye?

"No," she said aloud, unwilling to believe it. And then she recalled the sound she had heard. That meant he couldn't have gotten far. She was whirling around to try to head him off at the parking lot when she heard another noise, coming from inside the bathroom. Without a second's hesitation, she strode across the cabin floor and rapped boldly on the bathroom door.

The door opened, and Jess was face to face with the plump, perspiring countenance of Ann Jenkins. Mrs. Jenkins was clutching a scrubbing brush, and the odor of disinfectant pervaded the tiny room.

"Has Eth—Mr. Jamieson . . . checked out?" Jess asked in a choked voice, though it was all too obvious that he had. She felt as if she were dying.

"I'm afraid so, Miss Winslow. Hours ago. He got an urgent phone call from his office early this morning, and before you could say 'jackrabbit,' he'd settled his bill and arranged for a ride to Fort Bragg. I'm surprised he didn't let you know, but I guess he didn't want to wake you," Mrs. Jenkins said kindly. The growing friendship between Jess and Ethan had not gone unnoticed by the proprietress of Bill's Cabins.

Jess couldn't manage a reply. She was wondering if there had really been some crisis requiring Ethan's immediate return or if he had manufactured the whole thing to explain his sudden departure.

"Did he say if he'd be back?" she finally asked in a faint voice.

"I'm afraid not, dear. He told us he'd see us next year, so it doesn't seem likely he'll come back before then, does it? But I'm sure *you'll* be hearing from him, Miss Winslow. You have to remember he was in a terrible rush this morning."

Mrs. Jenkins's reassuring sympathy made Jess want to weep. But she discovered that there was something within her that refused to give way to despair. She couldn't let Ethan go out of her life without a fight. Slowly, a vague plan began to form in her brain.

"It's very upsetting that he would leave so suddenly, because—" Jess began hesitantly, "because he was intending to buy one of my paintings. We'd already agreed on a price. In fact he'd already paid me for it," she added as inspiration struck. "But now he's gone off without taking the painting he bought. I have his money, but he doesn't have the picture. And I won't feel comfortable spending the money until I know everything's squared away."

"That is a problem," Mrs. Jenkins said, wrinkling her brow in perplexity. "But I'm sure he'll get in touch with you about it soon. He wouldn't want to miss the chance of having one of your paintings, dear."

"The trouble is, he won't know how to reach me once I leave here," Jess confided desperately, wishing she were enough of an actress to sound casual. "I was hoping you could give me his address and phone number, so I could make sure he got the painting."

"I see. . . ." said Mrs. Jenkins a little dubiously, and Jess had the feeling that her shrewd, kind eyes saw a lot more than Jess had intended. "We usually don't give out that information, even to our other guests." She eyed Jess thoughtfully. "Still, this does seem to be a special case. All right, dear, come on down to the office with me, and I'll write out that address for you. And the phone number too."

*   *   *

Jess wondered why she'd never noticed how sinister a telephone could look. She stared balefully at the shiny black object that seemed to crouch menacingly on the table beside her bed. Tonight was her first night back in San Francisco, and she still hadn't found the courage to call Ethan.

She'd spent the last few days of her holiday in Mendocino working feverishly to complete one very special painting. At least she could work well again, now that she'd accepted her love for Ethan instead of trying to deny it. But she thought about him all the time and was obsessed with dread about what he would say when she made that telephone call. She was terrified that he would answer her with indifference or contempt. Could anything be harder for a woman than to call a hostile man and plead for his forgiveness and love?

So she'd ended up deciding, out of pure cowardice, to wait till she got back to San Francisco. As long as she put off calling, there was still hope. But if she called and Ethan told her he was through with her for good, how could she face it?

And now here she was alone in her apartment with the telephone, still too scared to stretch out her hand and dial one little seven-digit number. She'd already unpacked her suitcases, restocked the refrigerator, and washed the pile of dirty laundry she'd brought back from her trip. There were only two chores left to attend to—phoning Ethan and sorting the mail that had accumulated during her absence. Jess began sorting her mail. Very thoroughly.

She read every piece of junk mail and glanced at every page of the advertising circulars. She went through the bills and totaled up how much money she owed for the month. She read the note from her dentist reminding her it was time for a checkup. She fixed herself a cup of tea and read the long, newsy letter from her mother. The last envelope she opened was from the little art gallery where she occasionally sold her paintings, and the first thing she noticed was the check inside.

That was good news, but even better was the letter, forwarded along with the check, from the woman who'd bought her painting. The buyer wrote that she represented the Rande Smythe Gallery and wanted to see more of Jess's work. Would Jess be interested in discussing arrangements for the Rande Smythe Gallery to carry her paintings? If so, a phone number was included where Jess could get in touch.

It was just the boost Jess needed to restore her confidence. One word of interest and approval, and of course the prospect of future sales, was enough to make her start feeling good about herself again. Suddenly it didn't seem that Ethan might not forgive her. She picked up the phone and dialed his number.

The line was busy. Three minutes later, with hands shaking, she dialed again. Still busy. Two minutes later. Busy. Thirty seconds later. Busy. Jess gave a muffled scream and jumped up to start pacing around the apartment. "Why does being in love have to make me so neurotic?" she inquired aloud of the empty room.

She tried the number once more, but it was still busy. She grabbed her coat and picked up the flat, paper-wrapped parcel she had ready by the door. After running down three flights of stairs, she climbed into Old Betsy and headed through the fog-shrouded city toward an elegant residential area near the Presidio and overlooking the Golden Gate Bridge. On a narrow street lined with antique shops, she found a phone booth.

She was unprepared for the rush of panic and exhilaration that swept her at the sound of the phone's finally ringing. And when a deep, familiar voice answered at last, her throat felt so tight she could scarcely speak.

"Ethan, this is Jess," she said breathlessly. For a moment the silence on his end was so complete that she almost stopped breathing.

"Jess?" he said incredulously. "I'm . . . surprised to hear from you."

"I had to call, Ethan. I owe you an apology. For misjudging you and for letting my fears get in the way of seeing what kind of person you really are." Her voice gathered firmness as she went on. "And I should have been more honest about my feelings right from the beginning. I'm sorry." She hesitated. "Can you forgive me?" There was another long silence, during which she died a thousand deaths, and then at last he spoke, slowly and deliberately.

"That depends. Did you call me just to clear your conscience, or do you really want things to be different between us?"

"I want us to be friends again, only, this time I promise to be a better friend to you." She took a deep breath. "And I want us to be lovers, Ethan. If you still want me."

His reaction was immediate. "I'm on my way over."

"Wait!" she shrieked, half afraid he had already hung up.

"What?" he asked impatiently.

"Please stay where you are, Ethan. You see—"

"Why don't you want me to come over tonight?" he demanded curtly.

"Because I'm not calling from my apartment. I'm at a phone booth two blocks from your house."

"Dammit, Jess! Why the hell didn't you say so?" And he slammed the phone down. It had been Jess's darkest nightmare, when she was dreading making this call, that Ethan would hang up on her. But now that he had, she only laughed in jubilant relief, because she knew it meant he was on his way. Everything was going to be all right. She'd never thought she'd be glad to hear him say "Dammit, Jess!" in that exasperated, male way of his, but tonight it sounded like music to her ears.

She backed out of the phone booth and hurried along the sidewalk. Before she'd gone half a block, Ethan dashed around a corner and glanced from side to side as his eyes searched for her up and down the dark street. Then he spotted her, and Jess suddenly felt as if she and Ethan were two magnets being inexorably drawn together. The world around her blurred, and her only point of focus was Ethan's tall figure striding toward her.

His arms reached out to her, and for an instant his tiger-bright eyes devoured her face. And then she saw nothing more as they were wrapped together in a bone-crushing embrace, his mouth taking hers with a hunger that consumed them both.

"Come," he whispered urgently, and he held her tightly against him as he steered them up the steep street to the shelter and privacy of his home.

Ten

Jess took little notice of her surroundings as Ethan unlocked a door and led her up a long flight of stairs and into a lamplit room. All she could think of was his hard, lean body pressed against hers, flooding her with warm awareness and sweet desire.

"Jess, Jess, Jess," he murmured hoarsely, as he drew her down onto a couch piled with plump, soft cushions. He rained inflammatory little kisses across her brow and along her cheeks, while his hands fumbled with the buttons of her coat. When he removed it, his hands slid down her arms in one long caress from neck to shoulders to wrists. "My God, I've missed you so much," he whispered as he buried his face in the tendrils of bright hair against her neck.

"I've missed you too." She brushed her cheek against his silky dark hair, and her hands clung to his muscled shoulders as if she were a travel-weary bird come home at last to her roost. For a long moment they held each other, content just to be together, while their heartbeats mingled in a murmurous song of joy. The warm, muted colors of the room glowed in the lamplight. Outside the fog-blurred night pressed against the windowpanes but couldn't intrude. A foghorn sounded in the distance, making Jess feel intensely aware that the two of them were safe together in their circle of light in this room at the top of the stairs, at the top of a hill. It felt like the top of the world to her tonight.

And then Ethan kissed her with a long, sweet, slow, mind-drugging passion that seemed to melt the very boundaries of her being and merge her into one with him. Their lips and tongues spoke wordlessly of the deep emotions that overpowered them. When Ethan reluctantly pulled away, Jess felt as if a part of her had been severed.

"I want you to be sure about this," he said huskily. "Not like before."

"I'm sure, Ethan," Jess whispered, reaching out to capture both his wrists. Slowly she drew his hands toward her and lifted his open palms to place them against her breasts. "Just make love to me . . . *please.*"

"Is that an order?" he teased, while his hands lovingly cupped the rounded contours of her flesh. His thumbs moved simultaneously, one on each nipple, until the light friction of his touch had hardened them to tiny knots of pleasure swelling against the knit fabric of her sweater.

"You bet it's an order!" she responded breathlessly. "Though I did say please." She ran her hands up along the length of his thighs, relishing the feel of his steely strength tensing beneath the thin fabric of his dark trousers. As her hands stroked higher, she heard Ethan's quick indrawn breath, and her eyes lifted challengingly to meet the glittering, hungry promise in his tigerish gaze.

"I'll take those kinds of orders from you any time, lady," he drawled fervently. "Day or night." With one swift tug he removed her sweater, and two seconds later her bra was tossed after it. "Your breasts are like raspberries and cream," he whispered, surveying her with passionate reverence. And then he clothed her nakedness in the wet, silken depths of his mouth.

Jess gave a shivery moan of pleasure and eagerly arched her bare shoulders against the sofa cushions. The soft, velvety texture of the upholstery was like a sensuous caress along the smooth skin of her back, surrounding her on all sides with erotic stimuli.

Slowly Ethan unzipped her jeans, while his lips continued to suckle at her breasts. Smoothly he eased the worn denim down over her hips, thighs, calves, ankles, and toes, while his fingers brushed seductively against her warm skin. And then his hands began a long, lingering, intimate ascent back up to her waist. By the time his thumbs had come to rest on her hipbones and his fingers were splayed out across the small of her back, Jess felt almost delirious with pleasure.

Ethan lifted his head and gazed into her eyes. He trembled with awe and love at the knowledge that his touch had wrought this burning fever of need in her. Looking down at her flushed face, he let his fingers dip beneath the elastic band of her pastel-colored panties. Her lustrous, swollen red lips parted in a small "oh" of exquisite surprise at his rippling caress.

He fought to control the fierce, loin-scorching lust that gripped him as Jess arched her hips to allow him fuller contact with her moist femininity. He didn't want to rush things. Their pleasure would ripen and enrich itself with every second they held back. He forced himself to slow down as he removed the brief scrap of Jess's panties. He forced himself not to think of the warm, silken core of her womanhood now unveiled for him. But her parted thighs and soft, panting whimpers were almost impossible to resist. Somehow he had to lighten the pace, or it would be all over within seconds.

"Hey," he protested in a husky, teasing voice that was far from steady. "Aren't we forgetting something? I seem to be slightly overdressed for the occasion."

Jess's lashes flickered wide in surprise, and then

she gave a soft, breathless chuckle. "So you are. I should have noticed sooner, but I've been slightly distracted." Her mouth was soft with passion and tender laughter as she began to grapple clumsily with his shirt buttons. "Darn these buttons," she muttered impatiently.

"Want some help?" His voice was like a downy cloak of dark feathers sensuously enfolding her entire body.

"A fine help you've been so far!" she teased. "You've got me so dizzy and drunk with wanting you that I can't even undo a few buttons!" She displayed her trembling fingers. "You're worse than champagne!"

"At least I won't give you a hangover," he pointed out. Quickly, confidently, he took over the task of unbuttoning his shirt. He undid the first two buttons with ease, but then his movements slowed and his hand clenched and grew still as a strong tremor passed through him. He gave an involuntary groan of pleasure. "If I'm worse than champagne, you must be straight Scotch!" he accused the woman whose hands were busily invading the waistband of his trousers. Jess favored him with a misty smile of triumph.

Ethan bared his teeth at her and attempted to ignore the sensations of excruciating pleasure that her exploratory stroking aroused in his lower body. Impatiently his fingers clawed at the next shirt button, but his hand was slippery with perspiration and his concentration was irretrievably riveted on the way Jess's lips felt against his hipbone as she deftly removed his pants. "Damn these buttons!" he cursed.

"Want some help?" Jess drawled slyly.

"No, thanks." With a sudden dramatic gesture that sent buttons ricocheting into every corner of the room, he ripped the shirt open and fought his way free of its confining sleeves. Breathing hard, he gripped Jess by the shoulders. After a split second of startled silence, they both burst into incredulous laughter. "I don't believe I did that," he confessed.

"Neither do I." She bit her lip in an attempt to halt the laughter that bubbled out of her. "*This* is what I missed the most!" she exclaimed in sudden realization. "The way you make me laugh! Your sense of humor."

"Thanks a lot. Here I am holding you naked in my arms, about to make wild, crazy love to you, and you're telling me all you missed was my sense of humor!"

"You know that's not what I meant," she said with a reproachful smile.

"Yeah, I know." He was suddenly serious. "I missed it too. My sense of humor, that is. I thought I'd lost it permanently after the night you tried to run away from me. Nothing seemed very funny without you there to share it."

"Oh, Ethan," she whispered. "I'm so very, very sorry for what I put you through. I still can't quite believe you're willing to forgive me."

"I told you before, I'm not very good at holding a grudge. And especially not against you . . . my darling . . . Jess." His words were punctuated with deep, ardent kisses that sent arrows of ecstasy quivering through her aroused flesh.

"I don't deserve to be this lucky!" she gasped, feeling tears of happiness and relief gather in her eyes.

"True. You certainly don't," he agreed with teasing complacency. "It's a darn shame that a prize like me has to get thrown away on an ornery female like you."

"Oh, you!" She laughed through her tears. "Come here. I'll show you ornery!" She entwined her arms around his neck and drew his hard body close against her nakedness, opening her mouth to the hungry thrust of his tongue. Her hands kneaded the taut, slippery muscles of his back and buttocks, urging him to unleash himself into the wild sanctuary of her flesh.

He buried his face in the hollow of her neck, inhaling the aphrodisiac scent of her skin and hair. He brushed his lips over the fresh, flowery smoothness of her face. "Open your eyes," he breathed softly after he'd kissed her closed eyelids. Her lashes fluttered open, revealing green pools of liquid fire that beckoned him. He felt as if he were falling from a great height as he looked down into their mysterious depths. His breath caught in his throat. And then his body plummeted smoothly into hers, like a diver in search of sunken treasure.

Their love-making had the sure, fluid grace of a water ballet. Every rhythmic touch and movement had a resonance that awoke a thousand echoes in all the secret places of their flesh. It ended with a glorious reverberation that shook them both simultaneously, so that each shared in the almost impossible ecstasy that flowed through the other.

Afterward they lay joined together for long minutes of silent satisfaction, happy to be reunited at last in both flesh and spirit. Finally Ethan stood up and scooped Jess into his arms. "I'd better tuck you into bed. It's getting chilly out here."

"Mmm," she responded drowsily as he carried her down the hall. And then she remembered something she wanted to tell him. "You know what, Ethan?"

"No, what, Jess?" he asked indulgently.

"It wasn't your sense of humor that I missed the most after all."

"You mean it was my clarinet playing?"

"Mmm." Jess giggled and fell asleep.

Jess woke very early, and something was on her mind. Something was also lying heavily across her stomach—she smiled as she liberated herself from the warm pressure of Ethan's outflung arm. He was sound asleep.

With any luck, she could fetch the package from her car and be back before he woke up. She'd meant to give it to him last night, but then . . . last night had been complete as it was. They'd given themselves to each other, with no need for superfluous words and explanations or symbolic gestures of commitment. Their loving had been commitment enough. But today she wanted to put her feelings into words. And more than that—she had something to give Ethan that would, she hoped, speak even louder than words.

Her clothes were still in the living room, and Jess felt faintly ridiculous as she scurried, naked, down the unfamiliar hall in the cold gray light of dawn. Torrid passion seemed so improbable at this hour of the morning, she thought dryly. Her scattered garments on the Oriental carpet looked merely untidy— not romantically suggestive at all—and they felt slightly clammy against her skin when she put them on. But then she thought of Ethan's bare bronzed body sprawled across his bed, and the flame that burst alive inside her didn't stop to ask the time of day.

She adjusted the lock on the front door so it wouldn't latch behind her and then pushed her stiff legs into a brisk trot. It took her less than five minutes to reach her car, which was parked near the phone booth where she'd made her call to Ethan. She retrieved the brown paper-wrapped parcel from the back seat, locked her car again, and hurried back up the hill.

She'd been gone scarcely ten minutes, but still Ethan was waiting for her in the living room when she returned.

"Did you forget something?" His voice was harsh and wary, and his eyes burned like hot coals in his white face. His fists were plunged deep in the pockets of the long, navy blue, woolen robe he wore.

"Yes, I left this in the car last night—" she began, holding up the package, and then stopped abruptly as she realized what he meant. He was asking if she'd left something *here* and had come back just to claim it. "Did you think I had run out on you again?" she asked, horrified.

"Would it be so surprising if I did think that?" His voice was gruff. "You seem to make a habit of sneaking out of my bed and disappearing while I'm still asleep. Wouldn't it be a whole lot friendlier and more civilized if we both managed to wake up in the same bed together for a change?"

"You must know by now there's nothing friendly or civilized about me before my first cup of coffee in the morning!" she said in an attempt to make him smile.

"I remember." He smiled in spite of himself, but then his face turned bleak again. "That doesn't explain why you slipped out of here just now without a word."

"As I said, I wanted to get this from my car." She held the package out to him. "Here, take it. It's for you."

"For me?" He looked confused, and his hands seemed unsure of their grip as he took hold of the large, flat rectangular object. Jess held her breath as he awkwardly unwrapped it. Would he understand?

There was a long, long silence.

"Do you like it?" Jess asked tremulously, frightened by the tightness of Ethan's jaw. She couldn't see the expression in his eyes, because his head was bent so low that a lock of dark hair had fallen forward to hide the upper part of his face. "Please, say *something*, even if you think it's terrible!" she begged.

"I think—" He cleared his throat, and suddenly Jess realized that he was doing his damnedest not to cry. And he was failing. "It's beautiful, Jess," he said in a choked voice. He took two deep, quivering breaths and gave her a watery smile. "How could I not like a painting of my favorite place on earth, done by my favorite artist on earth?"

"I worked on it all last week," Jess told him shyly, fighting to hold back her own tears. "I even remembered to put the chimney in on your side of the cabin."

"So you did." He stared abstractedly at the painting for a second, and then, abruptly, he lifted his head and fixed her with his gaze. "Jess, I need to know—are you giving me this painting . . . to keep?"

"For as long as you want it," she answered fervently.

"And does that mean what I hope it means?" His voice was quiet, but Jess sensed the tension in him. He hoped, and yet he scarcely dared to hope. She stumbled over her words in her hurry to relieve him of uncertainty.

"It means . . . I trust you," she told him. "I trust you enough to give you this part of myself."

"I'm glad." The words were simple, but the look on his face was overpowering in its emotional eloquence. "Believe me, Jess, I'll treasure it always."

She took a deep breath, plunging on with what she'd planned to tell him, though she longed to put her arms around him and just let their bodies say it all. "And in case it needs to be said, Ethan, I'm trying to show you that I've stopped confusing you with any other man in my past. After Cliff vandalized the painting I'd given him, I swore I'd never make another gift like that to any man. But you're not just *any* man. And you're certainly not Cliff! So I'm through judging you by the things he did."

"Thank God." Carefully he set the painting down on the coffee table and enfolded her in his arms, pressing her tightly against him in a convulsive embrace.

"Once I got to know you, I didn't really believe you were all that much like him," she hastened to explain. "It's just that every time you touched me, I saw how helpless I'd be if you ever turned your sensual power against me. And that terrified me. I didn't feel ready to trust any man that much."

"And now?"

"Now I'm ready to start trusting you. Oh, I'm still scared when I think how different we are and how many things could go wrong. You're a wealthy businessman and I'm a not-yet-successful artist, so there are bound to be conflicts over our goals and expectations and lifestyles. But at least now I know you would never try to manipulate me the way Cliff did. You wouldn't use underhanded tactics to try to push me into doing things your way. And you've always been absolutely open and honest with me. I'm counting on that."

His body went oddly tense at her words, and the pressure of his hands was suddenly painful. A faint red flush scorched the tops of his cheekbones. Jess experienced a chill of disquiet. Why was he acting like a man stricken by a guilty conscience? And then his next question chased her thoughts in a new direction.

"Is that all we've got going for us, Jess? Trust?"

"It's a start, isn't it? But of course it's not—"

"Does that mean," he interrupted her harshly, "that it would be all over between us if I were ever dishonest with you?"

"Why? Are you planning on trying it any time soon? How do you expect me to answer a question like that?" she asked indignantly. "I'm certainly not going to tell you it's okay for you to lie to me!" Then she sighed. "But the truth is I'd probably forgive you for just about any stunt you pulled. Because I happen to be hopelessly in love with you."

"You are?" His eyes narrowed incredulously. And then he grabbed her by the shoulders and stared down at her as if she had the day's headlines printed across her forehead. "You are?"

"Yup." She wanted to smile up at him, but her face muscles suddenly felt all funny and her cheeks were suspiciously wet. "Surely you knew. I haven't exactly been able to hide the effect you have on me! In fact, the very first time we made love, you said you could *tell* I was in love with you. And of course I *was*, though I didn't know it yet."

"You told me I was deluding myself," he reminded her, and his expression made it clear that the memory still hurt. "You said all you felt for me was lust, not love."

"But you said you didn't believe me."

"Maybe not then. But after you ran away . . ."

"I've stopped running now, Ethan," she reassured him. "There was just no way I could go on fighting something as powerful as my feelings for you. I realized that the night I tried to barricade my door against you. The truth is, when I'm in your arms, I lose control." She smiled as she confessed her own vulnerability. "I can't resist you, so I've given up trying."

But Ethan had no answering smile. "You make me sound like some kind of disease," he said grimly. "A plague germ you were determined not to catch, but now that you're infected you plan on making the best of it and hoping for a speedy cure."

She stared at him, stunned and horrified by his unexpected bitterness. "It's not like that at all!" she gasped.

"Isn't it?" His jaw clenched. "What you've been telling me sounds more like a declaration of *lust* than a declaration of love. Basically you're saying you wouldn't be caught dead in a relationship with me if you had any choice in the matter, but because my talents as a bed partner are so overwhelming, you just can't help it!" His caustic tone was matched by the ugly curl of his lip. "I hope you don't expect me to feel flattered!"

"Dammit, Ethan, you're twisting everything I've said!" She was almost in tears at his accusations, but she was furious with him too. Why were they quarreling? Hadn't she just told him how much she loved him, needed him, wanted him? "What the hell is wrong with you?" she cried. "I love you, dammit!"

Finally her vehemence started to get through to him. His tortured gaze raked her face, and he began to realize how hurt and bewildered and angry she was.

"I'm sorry," he said wearily. "I'm acting like a damn fool. It's not your fault that love means something different to you than it does to me." His hold on her tightened once more. "I should be thankful just to have you here in my arms at all. What's the old saying—half a loaf is better than none? So what the hell am I complaining for?"

With a kind of desperate urgency, his mouth sought hers, finding and penetrating her lips with a fierce, probing heat. Jess's small gesture of protest was lost in the frantic energy of his onslaught, and she felt desire blaze up inside her like a spark exploding into flame in a tinder-dry forest.

But there was something she had to say before she could surrender to the dictates of passion. When the pressure of his mouth on hers eased slightly, she clasped his face between her hands and drew back far enough to speak.

"I *do* love you, Ethan," she insisted. "And it's not just physical, and it's not something I want to be 'cured' of, believe me!"

"I want to believe you," he assured her, searching her eyes with a probing, intense gaze. "Just keep saying the words and maybe they'll come true."

"They *are* true. I love you." She stretched on tiptoe to press her lips against his temple and the side of his jaw and then the contours of his ear. Her fingers glided through his sleep-tousled hair. "I love you." She whispered the words again, praying he would come to believe them in time even if he doubted them now.

"And God knows I love you," he responded in a harsh, fervent voice just before his mouth reclaimed hers in a hard, jolting kiss. Soon he was tugging her sweater off over her head, exposing the fact that she hadn't bothered to put her bra back on that morning.

Instantly he took one naked breast in his mouth, kneading it with his tongue until her whole body pulsed from his rhythmic suckling. His unshaven cheeks rasped against her soft flesh with a roughness that heightened her sense of his feverish, driving need. But it was her need, too, and soon she drew his mouth back up to her own, to meet the impassioned force of her kisses.

He carried her back to his room. Both of them were trembling, and, uttering low, feral cries, they seized each other. The electric impact of their joining ignited an explosive chain reaction that escalated uncontrollably.

Their bodies lunged and writhed with the effort to

overcome, at least for one euphoric moment, the doubts and uncertainties that still threatened to divide them. When the final release came, it was so sharp and intense it was almost painful.

Silence followed. They were both too moved by the shattering power of the experience they had just shared to be able to speak of it easily. But neither were they ready to talk of anything else. This heady, fragile sense of oneness would evaporate soon enough, and until then they had no desire to spoil the mood with words that might only lead to further misunderstandings. Before long, however, more mundane thoughts began to intrude.

It was Jess who finally broke the spell of silence. She gave a long, whooshing sigh of contentment. "Did I say it was your sense of humor I missed so much? Your playing of the clarinet, too?" she asked mischievously. "Well, I was dead wrong." She sat up and thrust her legs over the side of the bed so her feet touched the floor. "It was your green chili and jack cheese omelets."

"My what?" he asked with an affronted air.

"You heard me, Jamieson. I'm ready for breakfast. And you know how cranky I get if I don't have my meals on time."

"Oh, please, not that!" he gave a falsetto squeal of fake terror. "Anything but that! Whips, chains, squeaky chalk on a blackboard—I can take it all! But I can't stand to see you *cranky*."

Jess tried to whack him into insensibility with her pillow, but she was laughing so hard that her muscles seemed to have turned to jelly. Or maybe it was Ethan's laughter that had jellified them. The sight of his head thrown back in reckless merriment, so that his eyes brimmed with light and his grin split his whole face into lines of amusement and pleasure, made her feel dizzy with loving him.

Making good use of his own pillow, Ethan quickly fended off her attack and then pinned her to the bed as his lips demanded retribution. Jess was blissfully happy to oblige. When he lifted his head to gaze down at her a moment later, she was glowing and quivering with heat like the coals in the heart of a fire.

"That's funny. You don't look very cranky to me," he drawled, in a voice so warm and deep it sent a tremor along her spine. This time his kiss settled tenderly over her mouth, like a warm mist that crept softly between her parted lips. Each tiny lap of his tongue sent small currents of arousal whispering through her, fanning the flame within. "Is your heart set on eating that omelet any time soon?" he asked.

She shook her head.

"Good. Then I think I'll go take a shower," he announced, abruptly sitting up and stretching his arms. Jess glared at him furiously, ready to bring him down with a flying tackle if he put so much as one toe out of the bed. He gave her a bland, innocent smile. "Care to join me?"

"I thought you'd never ask."

It was well over an hour later when they finally sat down to devour green chili and jack cheese omelets at the dark oak table in Ethan's big, old-fashioned kitchen. But Jess wasn't complaining. It had been a very satisfying shower. And she hadn't felt one bit cranky the whole time.

"I love your apartment. Especially this kitchen," she informed Ethan as she sipped her coffee and gazed around the room, noting the leaded glass in the oak cupboard doors, the exposed brick of an old chimney that had been resurrected from beneath a layer of plaster, and the beautiful tile work on the counters.

"Thanks. I did a lot of the work on it myself when we converted this old three-story house into three luxury apartments instead of one impossibly large white elephant."

"Who's 'we'?" she asked carefully. "You said *we* converted it."

"I did it with a friend who does this kind of thing

for a living. As a matter of fact, he's the one in charge of the design and construction work on Fiori's Wine Gallery." He gave her a searching look and asked gently, "Did you think I meant Gina?"

Jess nodded and stared down at the empty cup in her hand. She wished she could pretend it didn't matter to her whether Ethan had ever planned to share this apartment with Gina. Or had they already been living here when Gina died? If that were true, Jess couldn't feel right about being here herself.

"I moved here about five years ago—a year after Gina's death," Ethan said quietly, as if he guessed what she was thinking. "Finding this place, planning the changes, and getting the work done were like therapy for me that first year. It helped get me involved in making a new life for myself. So don't think there are any ghosts for me here, Jess."

Once again she nodded, but this time she met his gaze directly and gave him a smile of quiet gratitude for his patience and understanding. It was a reassuring moment of closeness and communication for both of them, and that made it all the harder for Jess to understand what happened next.

Eleven

Ethan hesitated for a minute, and then he reached across the table and touched her hand. "I've been meaning to ask you, Jess. Are you ready to reconsider my offer to include your paintings in the opening exhibit of the Wine Gallery?"

"Reconsider? Why would I want to reconsider?" she asked in surprise.

"I thought you'd had a change of heart about me. Surely by now you realize I'm not Attila the Hun in a three-piece suit! So why won't you trust me enough to let me use your pictures in the gallery?"

It has nothing to do with whether or not I trust you, Ethan. I would accept your offer in a second if it weren't for our personal relationship."

"What does our relationship have to do with it?"

"Everything. The whole arrangement would smack of sexual favoritism."

"But it's not! Dammit, Jess, my feelings about your paintings aren't influenced by my feelings for you!"

She shook her head regretfully. "How can either of us be absolutely sure of that? It's tougher than you think to be completely objective about the work of someone you know. And just look at your past history when it comes to the women in your life—you can't deny you've shown a tendency to be over-protective. I don't want you playing that Lord Bountiful role with me! I don't want to be pampered and taken care of when it comes to my career. I just want to be taken seriously. It's terribly important to me to prove myself as an artist on my own merits, without any special favors."

"I can respect that. But what if I could arrange it so your paintings were anonymously screened by our artistic consultants? What if they gave your paintings an impartial and unbiased endorsement? Would that change your mind?"

Her mouth dropped open, and she stared at him. "You wouldn't try to influence them in any way?"

"I wouldn't even let them know I had any personal interest in their decision," he reassured her.

"Then—" It was on the tip of her tongue to tell him yes, she would gladly offer her work for consideration by the Wine Gallery consultants. But suddenly she remembered the most serious objection of all, and she groaned with disappointment. "It's no good, Ethan. No matter how scrupulously fair and impartial the selection process is, people won't believe it once they find out about us. If my paintings get into the exhibit, they'll say it's because I'm sleeping with the boss."

"Who cares what they think, so long as you and I both know we've done nothing unethical?"

"*I* care. It's my professional reputation we're talking about. It's my future. And you should care too, since the professional credibility of the Wine Gallery might be damaged if that kind of story got started."

"Surely you're exaggerating." He looked appalled. "Anyone in his right mind who sees your paintings is bound to recognize your talent as an artist. So why should people think you would need to sleep with anyone to get your work into a gallery?"

"Bless you for saying that," she said, deeply touched by his words of praise. But then she gave a slightly bitter laugh. "Unfortunately, people are all too ready to believe the worst, especially where a woman's achievements are concerned. If the critics got the idea that I was a rich man's dilettante mistress trying to use your money and position to buy professional recognition, they might not even bother to *look* at my work before they started cutting me to pieces!"

"I had no idea," Ethan said in a shocked voice, and Jess was surprised to see how tense and shaken he looked. Surely it wasn't all that important to him whether or not her paintings wound up in his gallery. "So you're saying," he asked hesitantly, "that it could actually *harm* your career if your paintings appeared in the Wine Gallery and it was generally known that you and I were romantically involved?"

Jess sighed. "It might. I just don't dare take the risk. Besides, I do have other options. Just yesterday I heard from another gallery that's interested in selling some of my stuff. All of a sudden everybody wants me!" she joked.

Ethan stiffened as if a dagger had been stuck between his shoulder blades. "No! You mustn't pursue that other offer," he cautioned urgently.

"Why on earth not?" The note of cold astonishment in her voice warned him that she didn't take kindly to his peremptory request.

"What I meant was . . . I'd rather you didn't. Please." He looked so tense and miserable that Jess didn't know what to think. Why should it matter to him? He didn't even know the name of this other gallery, yet he was already up in arms at the mere suggestion of its interest in her work. It didn't make sense.

Was his reaction just sour grapes? Had he wanted her paintings so badly for the Wine Gallery that he couldn't stand the thought of their appearing in the gallery of a competitor? That seemed unlikely. Or did his attitude stem from some hidden, unconfessed doubts he might still have about her artistic career? Would he be uncomfortable with any success she achieved that wasn't stage-managed by him?

The questions whirled through Jess's brain, but what good were questions without answers?

"Is there something you're not telling me?" she asked at last. "I've explained why my work can't appear in the Wine Gallery. Now will you please explain what difference it makes to you whether or not I follow up on this other offer from the Rande Smythe Gallery?"

He stared at her in absolute silence, while a stain of scarlet color surged and then receded in his cheeks, leaving them white as chalk. Jess thought she read a look of agonized indecision in his eyes, but then he turned his head away and the look was gone. His face tensed with sudden resolve, and at last he spoke, through lips so tightly pressed together they were edged with white.

"Just forget I ever said anything," he said. "I take it all back. You do what you think is best."

"Does that mean you won't object if I go ahead with it?" Jess asked hesitantly, baffled as much by his emotional intensity as she was by his rapid about-face.

"No, I won't object," he said in a suffocated voice.

"Then, why are you acting so upset?" Jess asked persistently.

"Because I'm not sure I'm doing the right thing!" he burst out. "In fact, I'm pretty darn sure I'm *not*," he added, more as if he were talking to himself than to Jess. "It was one thing to take a gamble when I didn't think I had anything to lose. I thought for once the end justified the means. But now . . . And it's not only my own neck I'm risking! Still, there are some dreams I can't give up."

Before Jess could summon up the presence of mind to close her gaping mouth and ask him what the hell he was talking about, Ethan turned on his heel and left the room.

When Jess found him a few minutes later, he was frowning in cross-eyed concentration as he attempted to knot his tie.

"Ethan?" she queried softly. "What's wrong?"

Deliberately he chose to misinterpret her question. "It's this damn tie! And I'm already late for work. The whole office has been in a state of crisis since old man Fiori wound up in the hospital with pneumonia last week, and we've all been working our tails off trying to share the extra load. Every minute I'm not there I'm letting people down. And my personal staff is under enough pressure as it is, with the Wine Gallery opening coming up in just a few weeks." He sounded angry with himself. "Hell, what *isn't* wrong?"

"Last night wasn't wrong," Jess answered him in a firm voice while her hands were at work straightening his tie. "And neither was this morning, though I'm sorry I helped make you late for work. I had no idea things were so hectic for you just now." She stood back to survey her handiwork. "*There*—your tie's not crooked anymore. And everything else will get straightened out eventually, you'll see."

"I'll keep trying to believe that," he said gruffly. "But hey . . . thanks for the pep talk." His smile was wistfully tender, but not convinced. He dropped a kiss on her brow and then turned his attention to putting on the vest and jacket of his pin-striped wool suit—this suit was even more formidable and expensive-looking than the one he'd been wearing the first time she saw him, Jess noticed.

"I suppose Mr. Fiori's illness was the reason you had to leave Mendocino so suddenly," she asked offhandedly.

"That's right. Though I was intending to leave that day anyway, as you may recall." As if she could forget! "I hoped you might come to your senses about us if I stayed away long enough for you to see how lousy it was being apart."

"But weren't you planning to stay away permanently? You *said* you were getting out of my life forever."

He gave her a long, hard look. "So now you know I'm not so trustworthy as you thought. I had all kinds of sneaky plans for seeing you once you got back to the city," he confessed without a trace of remorse.

"But you don't even know where I live!"

"Not true. All it took was a little snooping in Bill and Ann's guest book to find out your address and phone number. And you yourself told me the name of the temporary agency you work for. If you hadn't called me first, you'd have found me popping up in your path like a dandelion weed, wherever you went."

"Do you know, you're every bit as devious and unscrupulous as I ever thought you were!" Jess accused, admiration coloring her tone. "Luckily for you, I've always been rather fond of dandelions—such bright, cheery, determined little weeds! Of course I might have a different point of view if I were trying to preserve a perfectly groomed patch of lawn," she added judiciously.

Ethan's silence had an ominous quality. "I thought maybe that was what you *were* trying to do—preserve your own little patch of preordained, rigidly planned perfection. At the expense of any unauthorized person or emotion that inconveniently cropped up in your life. You're pretty ruthless when it comes to weeding out intruders."

He wasn't looking directly at her as he spoke the bitter, hurtful words. Instead he was busy putting his wallet and key case into his trouser pocket. He was carefully checking the contents of his hand-tooled leather briefcase. He was consulting his watch and striding toward the door.

"I've got to run," he announced.

"Whoa!" Jess cried, grabbing him by the back of his pin-striped suit coat and showing scant regard for the hundreds of dollars' worth of expert tailoring she was handling so roughly. "You can't throw that kind of condemnation at me and then just *run away*! We've got to get this cleared up!"

"Dammit, Jess! I'm late for work. I've got a *job* to go to, and I don't get *paid* to sit around having deep, meaningful conversations with my significant others! I don't have time for this!"

Jess snatched her hand away from him as if her fingers had been scorched. But she felt cold. Unbearably cold all over.

"I see," she said in a trembling voice. "I'm sorry I didn't realize how much your time must be worth! Obviously it's more than I could ever afford! Just ask your accountant to send me an itemized bill for all of it I've so inconsiderately wasted up to now, and then we can call it quits." Her voice broke on the last word.

"Dammit, Jess, you know I didn't mean it that way!" He caught her by the arm as she turned to flee, and he swore in frustration at the sight of the tears suddenly pouring down her cheeks. "Please listen to me! I'm sorry for the way I sounded, but I really do have to leave! Hell!" He pulled her against him and forced a hard, angry kiss onto her closed mouth. "We are *not* calling it quits, Jess! I promise you that." And then he was gone.

Half blinded by tears, Jess gathered up her coat and purse. Her eyes strayed to the painting lying on the coffee table in the living room, and she gave a shudder of agony as she remembered how high her hopes had been when she brought it to Ethan this morning. Everything had seemed so pure and simple then.

Now almost every certainty had been called into question, one way or another. She had been so sure she could trust Ethan, but now she sensed there was something dark and troubling that he was hiding from her. She couldn't trust him completely, after all. And he wasn't ready to trust her yet, either—he doubted her love and commitment. Worst of all, that final scene had stirred up her deepest fears about his businessman's priorities and values. His words had carried an underlying message, an unconscious assumption that his work was more important than their relationship simply because his job had a high monetary value. Or was she being overly sensitive? That was a definite possibility too. Jess sighed and dug through her purse to find a tissue to wipe her nose.

At least there were a couple of things she was still quite sure about. Ethan loved her. And she loved Ethan. No matter how many difficulties and misunderstandings had blown in like storm clouds during the night, still her heart was irrevocably committed to loving him. She was through letting vague doubts and apprehensions control her life. Somehow she and Ethan would work the problems out. She was no readier than he was to call it quits.

But the next move was up to him. Jess blew her small red nose defiantly, gave her painting a final hopeful glance, and let herself out of Ethan's apartment.

He called her at ten o'clock that night. "I'm still at work," he said. "Can I come see you tonight? We need to talk."

"Have you eaten?"

There was a short silence, as if her question had taken him by surprise. "No, but I thought I'd pick up a sandwich on my way over. If you're willing to see me, that is."

"I'm willing. Forget the sandwich—I've got some leftover homemade chicken soup I can heat up."

"Pardon me while I drool over the phone." He sounded almost like his usual self.

"Yuck! My advice is to just get your rear over here before it's past my bedtime, or you won't get any soup."

The soup was hot by the time he buzzed her apartment. Jess didn't say a word when she opened the door—she just went straight into his arms. His face was pale and weary, and there were lines of strain around his mouth and eyes.

Seated at the small table in the living room where Jess ate her meals, they didn't do much talking until Ethan had eaten two bowls of soup. The hot, chunky broth seemed to revive him, so he didn't look quite so exhausted.

"I'm sorry about this morning," he said at last. "I was feeling guilty and worried about work . . . and other things. I ended up saying things I didn't mean."

"You were right in terms of what you said about the way I tried to 'weed' you out of my life," Jess admitted. "But that's in the past. What hurt was the way you made it sound like I was still doing it. Please try to have a little more faith in me, Ethan. I know it's hard, after I was so unfair to you before, but do please try."

"I promise I'll try. And I won't make inflammatory remarks just as I'm stepping out the door," he promised ruefully. "And I certainly didn't mean to imply that my time was any more valuable than yours. It's just that I was getting slightly frantic about shirking my responsibilities to Fiori's."

"And I should have been more understanding about what a hurry you were in," Jess admitted. "So are we done with apologies for tonight?" she asked, smiling.

She was reluctant to question him about any of the other matters that still puzzled her, such as why he'd gotten so upset over the Rande Smythe Gallery's interest in her work. They would have to discuss those things eventually, but now was not the time. Both of them were tired, and the harmony between them still felt too fragile and tentative to risk disturbing it with probing questions. For now they needed to concentrate on the things that would bind them closer together, and forget everything that might pull them part.

"Oh, I think we've both apologized enough," Ethan said with a smile. "I had something a lot more pleasant in mind for us to do now."

"The best thing for you would be to get a good night's sleep," Jess felt it her duty to point out, however reluctantly. "You look like death warmed over."

"Thanks. You do a lot for my ego, Jess." He grinned.

"Don't worry, I have every intention of sleeping well tonight. And the best way to be sure of *that* is . . ." He got up from his chair and moved around the table.

"To go home and drink warm milk," Jess finished his sentence for him, right before he pulled her gently but firmly into his arms.

"Not quite," he said. His kiss was sudden and fiercely tender on her softly parted lips. Everything was blotted out except the taste and scent and texture of him, and Jess surrendered to the glorious invasion of her senses. "May I stay?" he asked softly, and she nodded. "You won't mind setting your alarm early enough so I can get home and change before work?"

This time she shook her head. "I won't mind. I have to be up early myself. I've got a new temporary office assignment starting tomorrow, and unfortunately it's way out in Walnut Creek."

"Then, what are we waiting for? The sooner we go to bed, the sooner we'll get to sleep. Right?" His hands were moving down her back in a slow, mesmerizing zigzag of sensation.

"If you believe that, you're not half as smart as I thought you were," Jess murmured as he stepped backward in the direction of her bedroom door, pulling her with him in a close, intimate embrace. His low, resonant chuckle was like a warm, titillating caress.

They made love carefully, tenderly, as if their bodies were especially delicate and vulnerable tonight. As if the doubts and misunderstandings that had bruised their spirits had also left unseen bruises on their naked flesh. Their lovemaking was a healing balm soothed over them, and suddenly it seemed easy to hope. Surely their relationship was finally on the upward path. All they needed was time to resolve their doubts and questions.

But time turned out to be one thing they had a very short supply of. The biggest culprit was Ethan's job, especially his work on the Wine Gallery. Everything would be different once the big opening had taken place, but in the meantime he had to work late, night after night. Only once in a while did he manage to spend time with Jess afterward.

Always on these occasions he looked so tired that Jess felt guilty just for keeping him awake. It certainly never seemed like the right time to have a deep, probing discussion of his possible hang-ups about her career.

Their hours together were too few and too precious to waste in unpleasantness, especially when it was so much easier to spend them in laughter and loving. Jess even quit mentioning the successful progress of her negotiations with the Rande Smythe Gallery, because she couldn't bear to see the perceptible stiffening in Ethan's manner every time the subject came up.

So the weeks slipped by, and despite the hours of closeness Jess and Ethan managed to share, it seemed to Jess that in many ways they remained strangers to each other. She felt as if she were only on the fringes of his life. After all, she'd never met his family, his friends, or his co-workers. She hadn't even been to his apartment again since the first time. Of course, all that was just because he was too busy for socializing right now, and naturally he preferred that it be just the two of them, since they had so little time together anyway. But still . . .

Not that she had any great hankering to eat in fancy restaurants or rub shoulders with the upper crust at posh gatherings. Jess preferred the meals she shared with Ethan in her apartment or at the various small, out-of-the-way eateries featuring fabulous food that Ethan had such a talent for discovering. And she loved the way they'd spent their one free afternoon together, when they rented bicycles and pedaled their way from one end of Golden Gate Park out to the ocean beach at the western end. But she did begin to wonder exactly what role

Ethan intended her to play in his life. Was she just to be a back-street mistress to him?

Stop being so melodramatic, she scolded herself. You know what you are to Ethan—you're the woman he loves! But then, why did he seem to be keeping their relationship a secret from the rest of the world? Could he possibly be . . . ashamed of her? Reluctantly she remembered Beryl's hysterical accusations. "I'm not good enough for fancy hotels and mixing with important people, am I?" the other woman had said. "I'm just the girl you take to a cheap old shack in the middle of nowhere!" Could Beryl possibly have been right about Ethan's attitude toward women who weren't in his social class?

But that was ridiculous! Ethan was hardly a snob. He'd genuinely loved the simple, casual life in Mendocino. And now he was simply choosing to relax in that same easygoing, unfancy style here in San Francisco. Who could blame him for not wanting to get dressed up and make small talk after the long, grueling hours he put in at work? Jess felt silly for letting her own insecurities and overly sensitive imagination come up with such nonsensical notions.

But that was before the morning she opened her newspaper to the "People" section and discovered Ethan's photograph. He was one of several smiling faces in a group of attractive people wearing evening clothes and holding cocktail glasses and conversing brightly for the camera. The caption identified the event as a fund-raiser for the symphony orchestra, and noted the names of the illustrious guests pictured. Including one Ethan Jamieson III.

"Mr. Jamieson the *third*, please," she demanded as she strode up to the receptionist's desk on the second floor of Fiori's administrative headquarters. She'd been surprised to find that their offices were located in a beautifully restored block of ornate Victorian row houses converted into a single office building—hardly the towering, impersonal edifice of glass and steel she'd been envisioning all this time. But she was in no mood right now to appreciate the architectural charms of Ethan's workplace.

"Do you have an appointment, Miss—?" the receptionist asked in a professionally amiable tone, though one swift glance at her desk calendar must have informed her that Mr. Jamieson had not been expecting this very determined-looking young woman.

"My name is Jessica Winslow, and I have reason to believe Mr. Jamieson will see me without an appointment," Jess insisted. *Mr. Jamieson had damn well better see me*, she thought. "The matter is urgent," she added aloud.

"I'm sorry, but he's in a meeting right now and doesn't wish to be disturbed," the other woman answered with a smooth, apologetic smile. "If you'd care to wait, I'll let him know you're here, just as soon as the meeting breaks up. But I can't guarantee he'll see you—he's terribly busy. Perhaps if you wished to make an appointment?"

"No, I'll wait in his office," Jess announced, sprinting around the desk and opening the oak-paneled door behind it before the receptionist could do more than gasp in horror. Jess knew very well that she was committing a major faux pas, but she was too stubbornly angry to care. She might have had second thoughts, however, if she'd realized that Ethan's meeting was taking place right on the other side of the door she was so impulsively entering.

Half a dozen pairs of startled eyes turned to stare at her in disapproving astonishment. Half a dozen brows furrowed with ill-concealed impatience as the group waited for her to explain what she meant by barging in like that. It was an intimidating sight, but not nearly so intimidating as the look of utter fury that shimmered in the seventh pair of eyes. Eyes of gleaming gold barred with black. Ethan didn't even know why she was here, but he certainly wasn't happy to see her. Jess swallowed the lump in her throat and tried to think of something to say.

At that moment her arm was firmly grasped from

behind by a burly security guard. The receptionist really must have pushed the panic button, Jess thought wearily. She suddenly felt more miserable than angry. What had she hoped to accomplish by staging this confrontation with Ethan?

"That won't be necessary, Larry," Ethan instructed the security guard in clipped tones. "If our visitor's business with me can wait another ten minutes, have her sit in that vacant office down the hall while we finish up here."

Though he didn't address her directly, Jess answered the implied question. "Yes, I can wait, Ethan," she said. Eight pairs of eyes, including the security guard's and the receptionist's, shifted rapidly from Jess to Ethan and back again, and now those eyes were full of curiosity and speculation.

By the time Ethan entered the room where Jess had been pacing for the last fifteen minutes, his anger appeared to be under control, though his expression was still one of disgruntled chilliness.

"What's wrong, Jess? What was so urgent that you had to rush over here without taking the time to phone?"

"*This,*" Jess said grimly, shoving the newspaper at him. He glanced down at it, puzzled, and then his eyes found the target of her pointing finger. His quick, involuntary intake of breath was audible. "You told me you had to work that night," Jess reminded him in a tight, painful voice.

There was dead silence, and Ethan's face went white. "It was a social obligation," he finally said quietly. "I didn't go there to have a good time."

"But it still wasn't exactly *work.* I could have come along if you'd wanted me to. It would have been a chance for us to spend a few extra hours together. But you never asked. You just said you were working. *Why,* Ethan? Is it because you're having second thoughts about our relationship? Is it because you don't think I'll fit in with your friends?"

"*No!*" He sounded absolutely shocked. "It's nothing like that!"

"Then, why? I'm sure I'm not imagining this. Something is definitely wrong. Why don't you want anyone to know about us?" Her eyes beseeched him to offer an explanation that would make it all right again.

He groaned and turned away. "I can't tell you right now," he said in a tortured voice. "Please just trust me—or rather, give me time." He stumbled over the words. "The Wine Gallery's grand opening is only two days away. I give you my word that I'll explain everything then."

Already Jess was shaking her head in angry despair. There were too many unanswered questions in their relationship. What right did he have to make her wait for an explanation at his convenience, just because he was too busy with work? She was tired of living with all these doubts and shadows between them. She needed reassurance now.

He saw the refusal written on her face, and desperately he tugged her into his arms. "I swear it has nothing to do with the way I feel about you!" he told her.

"Then, prove it," she said. "Show me there's a legitimate place for me in your life." She gazed up into his troubled, tawny eyes, and issued her challenge: "And you can start by inviting me to attend the opening of the Wine Gallery with you!"

His look was inscrutable as he considered her suggestion for a long, tense moment. And then he gave an odd, reckless little smile. "All right," he said, and his arms tightened on her back and shoulders. "But first I want to know if I have a legitimate place in *your* life. Don't you think it's time you made some sort of commitment of your own?"

Her pale green eyes were baffled. How much more committed could any woman possibly be?

"Marry me, Jess?" he murmured.

Twelve

She tried to hide the reckless joy that sprang to life inside her at his words. Even though her first instinct was to tell him yes, she would gladly be his wife, still she knew they had a lot to talk over first. After all, it wouldn't be right to commit themselves to marriage while Ethan still doubted the strength of her love or while she was still worried that he was hiding something important from her. And his odd behavior over the past few weeks still had to be explained.

"I can't give you an answer yet," she said gently. "You've asked me to wait for your explanation—don't you think it's only fair that we postpone our discussion of marriage until then as well?"

"It may be fair, but I don't like it," he said bluntly. "Either you love me enough to marry me or you don't. Why can't you just tell me now which one it is?"

"I do love you, Ethan," she said in a constricted voice. "It's just . . . we need to get our relationship straightened out a bit better before we talk about marriage. Marriage should start with openness and communication, and we don't have too much of those yet, do we?"

"No, not yet," he admitted grimly. "Dammit, Jess! I can't bear the thought of losing you!"

"Then, don't waste your time thinking about it!" she advised him with a hint of tender mischief in her smile. "It's not very likely to happen."

"But you don't know what—Oh, never mind," he interrupted himself, looking tense and miserable. "I'll explain everything the night of the Wine Gallery opening. And I just hope to God you'll understand."

"I'll do my best," she promised gravely.

They arranged that he would pick her up at eight on the evening of the opening and then he kissed her good-bye. It was an oddly troubling kiss, one that seemed full of desperation and sadness, and Jess didn't know quite what to make of it.

As it turned out, Ethan did not come by her apartment at the appointed time two days later. Instead he sent a chauffeured limousine, and the uniformed chauffeur handed her an envelope containing a hastily scrawled message from Ethan.

"I meant to see you tonight before the opening to try to explain," he had written, "but a last-minute emergency has me all tied up. Please let Joe drive you to the Wine Gallery, and I'll meet you there. And please, Jess, try to understand and forgive. All my love, Ethan."

Jess gave a puzzled little smile. Of course she was disappointed that she and Ethan couldn't arrive together after all, but surely he didn't think she was so unreasonable as to hold that against him. She knew he had a lot of responsibilities and was under a lot of pressure tonight, so it was easy to "understand and forgive." But still, it was sweet of him to apologize so profusely.

Jess felt as if all eyes must be watching her when Joe helped her out of the sleek black limousine in front of the brightly lit entrance to Fiori's Wine Gallery. She was glad now that she'd splurged so madly on her dress for the evening—a long, shimmering gown of sea-foam green that left her shoulders bare. She held her head proudly erect beneath the elegantly coiffed abundance of her upswept hair. Ethan wasn't waiting for her at the door, so Jess walked in alone.

The larger, grocery-oriented section of the store was closed off for the night, and all the revelers were gathered in the new Wine Gallery section. A small jazz ensemble was playing in the far corner, and music and talk and laughter eddied around Jess as she stood on the fringes of the party, gazing at what Ethan had created. It was hard to get any clear idea of what the room might actually look like when it wasn't crowded with men and women in evening clothes, but Jess saw enough to know that the Wine Gallery was everything Ethan had promised, and more.

She had a quick impression of a variety of surfaces— mellowed brick, gleaming natural wood, and pristine white. Through the maze of people, she caught brief, tantalizing glimpses of the artwork on the walls, lit by strategically positioned track-lighting fixtures. Wine racks were unobtrusively placed around the room, their four-foot height not detracting from the impact of the artwork. It was all absolutely beautiful, and Jess could hardly wait to find Ethan and tell him he was a genius.

And then a knot of people off to her right shifted slightly and she got a good look at a large painting their bodies had shielded from her view. Oddly enough, it took a split second before it registered in her brain that the reason that particular canvas looked so familiar was that she herself had painted it. She moved in slow motion across the floor to stare up at the painting that should have been on display at the Rande Smythe Gallery, several miles away. Her name, the painting's title, the date of its completion, and an astonishingly high price were all neatly printed on a card below the work. And then, as she glanced at the walls on either side of her, she saw several more of her paintings there.

Her thoughts circled wildly for a second or two and then zeroed in at full speed on the obvious target—Ethan Jamieson III. It took no time at all to realize that the offer from the Rande Smythe Gallery had been bogus—just a smoke screen to hide where the real offer was coming from. Their "representative" had in reality been working for Ethan, and the paintings Jess thought she'd placed with the other gallery had been destined all along for Fiori's Wine Gallery.

Jess felt as if she'd been hit in the solar plexus. Ethan had known exactly what her wishes were on the subject, yet he'd deliberately chosen to go behind her back to trick and mislead her. Oh, he'd had a few attacks of conscience along the way, as well he might! But that hadn't stopped him. No wonder she'd suspected he was hiding something from her. But she'd never suspected anything like this.

To think that only two days ago he'd pleaded with her to trust him. *Trust him!* She had to get out of this place before she broke down.

Jess turned quickly and began to dodge her way through the crowd. Her mounting sense of urgency was suddenly thwarted at every turn, by white-coated waiters carrying trays of wineglasses, by a woman in a long black dress who took an unexpected step backward and spilled her drink, and by what seemed hordes of other people determined to cross the room in the opposite direction from the one Jess was attempting to take.

Just as she escaped at last out into the cold, revivifying air of the parking lot, Jess felt a hand on her arm, and a hoarse voice spoke her name. She spun around to confront the fear-shot eyes and emotion-ravaged face of the man who'd just destroyed all her newborn hope and trust. In his elegant black evening clothes and dazzlingly white shirt, he looked like a stranger.

"How could you, Ethan?" she asked brokenly, and

her green eyes were huge and accusing in her pale face.

"I didn't mean for you to find out this way. I meant to tell you before you got here, to explain—"

"I don't see that it would have mattered," she said in a cold, tight voice. "Up in Mendocino you spent days wearing down my defenses, teaching me to trust you, getting me to open up my heart to you. You made me feel guilty for ever having doubted you! In the end I gave you all the love and trust I had to give. And for what, Ethan? So you could deceive me?"

"It's not like that, Jess, I swear it!" he protested, and then belatedly realized that they were the object of several curious glances. "Let's talk in the car," he said urgently, and Jess let him lead her away from the bright lights and people near the Wine Gallery entrance. What was the point of making a scene? It wouldn't solve anything.

Joe, the chauffeur, was smoking a cigarette and playing solitaire in the front seat of the limo. "Just keep driving around the block till I tell you to stop," Ethan instructed him as they climbed into the back.

"You may as well tell him to drive me home," Jess said numbly.

"Dammit, Jess, please listen to me!" All she could see of him in the darkness inside the car was the pallor of his face and the snowy white of his shirt-front, contrasted against the utter blackness of his hair and his evening jacket. But hearing his voice was like reading the desperation in his eyes. "Please try to understand. I know it was wrong of me to deceive you. But first you wouldn't do it because you thought the Wine Gallery would be some kind of tasteless rip-off; I think I persuaded you that wasn't true. Then you were afraid I wasn't being objective about your paintings, that I was letting my personal feelings for you affect my decision. So I came up with the idea of letting my artistic consultants decide whether your work would be included or not, and that *is* how your paintings were selected, by the way. It was a completely unbiased decision."

He took a deep breath, and then went on. "But it was your final objection that really had me worried. You said if our names were linked romantically, it would put your professional reputation in jeopardy to have your paintings appear in my gallery. That threw me for a loop, and at first I tried to undo what I'd already started when I first returned from Mendocino. All in a panic, I asked you to refuse the offer I'd set up from the Rande Smythe Gallery. But of course you wanted an explanation. And that was when I made the decision to go ahead with my plans after all. I figured if nobody knew about our relationship, it would be safe for you to display your work in the Wine Gallery, and I made up my mind that our feelings for each other would be the best-kept secret in town."

"I see. So that's why you've spent the last few weeks sneaking around like a married man involved in a clandestine affair. And that's why you were so angry with me for coming to your office. It was all for my own good." Her voice was full of bitter irony. "But you still haven't explained the purpose behind it all. You haven't told me *why.* What was so important about having my paintings in your damn gallery that you felt justified in duping and deceiving me?"

"Jess, you know I've wanted *you* ever since the night we met. What you never guessed was that I felt the same way about your paintings—I wanted *them* for the Wine Gallery. The minute I saw them, I *knew.* You see, I already had this vision in my head, this dream of what the gallery could be like. When I saw your paintings it was like finding the key to the realization of that dream. And after that, I wasn't willing to compromise. Even when you refused to let me use your work, I couldn't accept that decision as final, because I saw that you were tempted by the offer. That led me to hope that if only I could find solutions to the valid objections you'd raised, then you'd forgive me once it was a successful *fait accompli*. I thought you might even be pleased."

His voice was low and pleading in the shadowy interior of the limousine, but Jess turned her head away. "You were wrong," she said. "I can't forgive you for this. You sacrificed my wishes, you gambled with my good name, and you forfeited my trust, all for the sake of your business interests!"

"Jess—"

She pounded feverishly on the glass panel separating them from the driver's seat. "Stop the car!" she shouted, and as the vehicle slowed, she put her hand on the door handle. "I'll take a cab home," she announced through clenched teeth.

"Over my dead body." The words were spoken in a low, dangerous growl, and his hand closed over her wrist like a vise as the limousine came to a complete stop. "Is there nothing I can say that will make you forgive me?" he demanded, searching her set face in the harsh light from a nearby streetlamp.

She shook her head in mute, furious denial.

"Then, I guess this is good-bye. It's too late now to change what I've done." The stark finality of the statement cut through the unraveling threads that had bound them together, and Jess felt like a boat without compass, cut adrift and left to the mercy of an uncharted, empty sea. "I'll tell Joe to drive you home."

Jess attempted some small, choking reply, and suddenly Ethan gathered her into his arms and implanted a brief, disturbing kiss on her trembling lips. "I just want you to know," he whispered, "I would never have done it if I'd guessed how much it would hurt you. And if I'd known the choice was between having you or having your paintings, I'd have chosen you." And then he pulled away, and Jess heard the slam of the door and the purr of the big car's engine as it carried her away and left him standing there under the streetlight.

*   *   *

Jess tried to pretend that Ethan's parting words and the touch of his lips hadn't turned her mood to one of regret. She wanted to feel only anger. Hard, clean, self-righteous anger. Ethan had thought he could have his cake and eat it too. He'd arrogantly assumed he could betray her trust and then find quick and easy forgiveness. Now he knew how wrong he'd been.

But the long, agonizing hours of that night taught Jess that she had been wrong as well. Forgiveness did not come quickly or easily, but still, it came. Slowly, like water seeping through porous rock. Bit by bit, like the pieces of a jigsaw puzzle fitting together to create a whole. By the time the gray morning light penetrated her apartment to find her huddled in an armchair by the bedroom window, Jess had reached a dawning awareness of her own.

When she first learned what he'd done, it had seemed to justify every crazy fear and prejudice she'd ever had against him. It had been wrong of him to keep her in the dark about what he was doing. But his decision hadn't been made lightly—she'd seen him agonize over it on their first morning together in San Francisco. And he *had* been careful and considerate of her welfare in the way he'd done it. But most important of all were his reasons for doing it in the first place. And they were very surprising indeed.

She remembered the things he'd said and the words he'd used to describe his feeling about the Wine Gallery. Words like "vision" and "create," "dream" and "ideal." Jess realized with a shock that they were exactly the kind of words an artist might use. To Ethan, the Wine Gallery was his creation, his inner vision brought to life, his dream become reality.

And all this time . . . She'd been so busy jumping to conclusions about him that she'd never even guessed how alike they were. It was true that Ethan wore three-piece suits on occasion and successfully wielded more financial power than Jess could even shake a stick at. And he had to possess ambition and an astute business sense or he'd never have gotten where he was. But his fundamental values—the things he cared about and thought worth striving for—were very similar to her own. Yet all this time she'd assumed there was a gaping chasm between them that never could be fully bridged!

She jumped purposefully out of the chair, only to discover that her legs were cramped and stiff from sitting so long. She rang Ethan's number, but there was no answer. She let it ring a dozen times before she gave up, and then she called his office. Even though it was a Saturday, some unfortunate soul was slaving away there, and he informed Jess that Mr. Jamieson wasn't in and, so far as he knew, wasn't expected in at all that weekend. The Wine Gallery, which she tried next, was open for business and deluged with customers, but no, Mr. Jamieson himself wasn't in the store. Nor was he expected.

After trying his apartment again, she tried to think where else he might be. Instinctively she thought she knew the answer, but she picked up the phone again and dialed the number for Bill's Cabins, just to be sure she wasn't setting off on a four-hour drive for nothing.

At first the news was bad. No, Mr. Jamieson wasn't there. But yes, he *was* expected. And yes, the room next to his was still available. Twenty minutes later, Jess and Old Betsy were headed north across the Golden Gate Bridge, bound for Mendocino.

The early darkness of a December evening had already closed in by the time Jess hauled her suitcase and a bag of groceries into Bill and Ann's tiny office to sign their guest book and take possession of her room key. She should have felt exhausted after the long drive, having had so little sleep the night before, but she was too excited and hopeful to be tired. And the cold, fresh scent of the sea and the sound of its restless movement stirred her heart with memories.

"Welcome back, Miss Winslow," Ann Jenkins greeted her, adding a friendly wink. "We haven't said a word to you know who about your coming here, because we didn't want to spoil your little surprise. The poor man sure looks like he could use some cheering up!"

"That's what I'm here for . . . I hope," Jess said with a smile. She wouldn't let herself even think of the possibility of failure.

Bill Jenkins gave her a hand with her suitcase and unlocked the cabin door for her, and then left her alone with the memories that crowded round her. Quickly she unpacked the bag of groceries she'd purchased in Mendocino, and set to work with a knife and cutting board. When the pot of homemade fish chowder was simmering gently on the stove, she dashed into the bathroom for a quick shower. She almost broke into her old habit of singing under the spray, but luckily had the brains to catch herself just in time. Her inability to carry a tune would have been a dead giveaway to the man next door.

She rushed to the stove to stir the chowder, and then rushed to the bed to unpack some necessary items from her suitcase. One was a jade-green pajama outfit of quilted silk, which plunged low across her breasts and hugged her curves with a flattering grace. She'd bought it the day Ethan proposed, thinking of it as something for their honeymoon. But better to make sure there *was* a honeymoon than to hoard it like miser's gold.

The last thing she unpacked was her portable electric hair dryer. And then she turned on every light in the room, opened the refrigerator door, pushed down the toaster, and, finally, turned on the hair dryer.

"*Hey!*" came a hoarse shout from the other side of the wall, and then the room went black. Carefully muffling her voice with her fist, Jess gave an artful shriek.

"Are you all right over there?" the voice next door

demanded impatiently. Jess didn't say a word. "Oh, *hell*!" the man swore in a low but audible undertone. There were some thuds as he made his way across the floor, and then his footsteps tramped loudly on the plank walk outside. Without bothering to knock, he thrust open the unlocked door and stepped into the room.

"Dammit, lady, didn't they tell you not to use your hair dryer here?" he bellowed as he shone his flashlight around the room, trying to locate a human presence. "Where the hell are you, anyway? Are you okay?"

Jess gave a muffled giggle. She couldn't help it. Ethan turned sharply at the sound, and as Jess stepped out from behind the bathroom door, feeling very wanton and sultry with her hair down and the jade-green silk outfit clinging to her bare flesh, the flashlight beam caught her right in the eyes. Blinded by its glare, she tried to step forward and promptly tripped over a chair leg. What should have been her big, dramatic entrance turned into a shambles as she went sprawling across the floor.

"Aughh," she moaned, clutching her bruised shin. The dark, shadowy figure behind the flashlight seemed frozen in shock for a second, but then he dropped to his knees on the floor beside her.

"Jess?" he whispered in wonder and disbelief. "Jess, are you all right?" He set the flashlight down and reached out to her with an oddly tentative gesture, as if he expected her to pull away at any second. But Jess let him take her by the shoulders and gently lift her until her head was resting against the solid comfort of his chest. "Where does it hurt?" he asked softly.

"My leg. But it'll be okay. It's only my sense of dignity that's terminally wounded."

"Let me see it," he insisted.

"What—my sense of dignity? I'm afraid it doesn't even exist anymore."

"No, Miss Smart-ass, your *leg*." So she peeled back the silky fabric of her trouser leg, and then moved his fingers to the place where the bump was forming. Just the touch of his fingertips along her bare ankle made her forget the pain, as a very different sort of sensation went fluttering its way to her central nervous system.

"I'll get some ice to keep the swelling down," Ethan said gruffly, but Jess knew by the catch in his breathing that he, too, had been affected by that brief, light contact.

He helped her up off the floor and gently settled her on the edge of the bed before crossing the room to the kitchen area. "What's your refrigerator door doing open?" he asked in surprise as he rummaged through the freezer compartment searching for an ice-cube tray.

Jess knew she couldn't think up a good answer to that, so she didn't even try. "As long as you're up, would you mind stirring that pot of chowder on the stove?" she asked, lying back against the pillows at the head of the bed.

"Chowder?" He swung the flashlight around to study the expression on her face. After a brief, silent exchange of glances he turned back to his task. He didn't say another word until several minutes later, when the chowder had been stirred, the oil lamp on the table had been lit, and a pack of ice cubes had been wrapped up in a dish towel and carefully applied to the swelling on Jess's shin.

Jess sensed the gathering tension in him as he pulled up a chair beside the bed and sat down. With his legs braced far apart, he leaned toward her and rested his muscled forearms on his thighs. His shadowed eyes were probing, yet seemed fearful of what they might find.

"Don't you think it's time to put me out of my misery and tell me why you're here?" he asked with quiet intensity. "Why the chowder? And why did you deliberately blow the fuse?"

Jess gave him an impish smile. "Can't you guess? I heard there was a 'poor, lonely, rich bachelor' next door, and of course I wanted to be the first to swoop in like a vulture and take my pickings." Ethan winced as he recognized the echo of his own words from their very first encounter. "After all," Jess continued, "it's not every day that some woman is dumb enough to walk out on a man like you, so we vultures have to snatch at every chance we get. I figured you'd have to come rescue me when the fuse blew. And I've heard that you're very susceptible to homemade fish chowder."

"Dammit, Jess! You know I'm *susceptible* . . . to just about everything you do! I'm so susceptible I'll go crazy if you don't tell me in plain English whether or not you've forgiven me!"

"Once you explained to me that you were just no good at holding a grudge." Jess smiled ruefully. "Well, I happen to be *great* at holding a grudge, but in your case all I could manage were a few hours of it."

"And why was that?" he asked, never taking his eyes off her face.

"Because I love you so damn much. And because it finally dawned on me that what you did wasn't done out of any desire to manipulate me, or out of any obsession with money or power or success. Oh, you were obsessed, all right, but what you were obsessed with was the drive to create something beautiful. And since that's an obsession I happen to share, I can hardly hold it against you!"

"I tried to tell you that last night—"

"I know, but I was too angry to listen." Jess reached up to caress away the worry lines that creased his forehead. "After all, how could I stay mad at you, when we have so much in common? The two of us belong together. You're sneaky and devious, and I'm cranky and ornery and unreasonable—obviously, we're a perfect match!"

"It took you long enough to figure that out," Ethan said huskily as he leaned forward and kissed her with taut, hungry relief. Jess's mouth welcomed him, and each moist thrust of his tongue was a poignant and passionate reminder of what they had almost lost.

She sighed with pleasure as his hands coursed over the smooth fabric of her pajama outfit, warming the glossy silk that lay against her bare skin like a cool, scented layer of flower petals. Soon she felt the hard weight of his body shifting as he settled himself beside her on the bed, and she turned her head so their faces were almost touching.

"Are you ready to talk about marriage now, Jess?" Ethan asked softly.

"*Yes,*" she breathed, wondering why his eyes were still so troubled.

"You said just now that we belong together." He spoke the words as if he cherished the sound of them, and then he went on, more hesitantly. "I'm hoping that means you've begun to think of me the way I've always thought of you. As someone you would *choose* to love. Someone you feel committed to. Someone you want to share your life with. Someone you want to marry." Before Jess could answer, he added, with a trace of bitterness, "Not just someone whose touch you can't resist. Not just someone you love because you can't help it!"

"But I *can't* help it!" she protested, laughing. She turned quickly sober at the sight of Ethan's stricken expression, however. "Oh Ethan, I feel *all* those things for you. Don't you know that every bone in my body is committed to loving you? And so is every cell of my brain and every beat of my heart. And I definitely want to marry you!"

All the breath in his body seemed to whoosh out in one long sigh of happiness and relief. "Glory hallelujah," he whispered, and then he kissed the curve of her cheek, the tip of her nose, the quivering softness of her closed eyelids. At last his lips descended to her mouth, savoring it as if their kiss were a shared cup of ceremonial wine, a pledge, and a promise of their future together.

"I still can't quite believe this is really happening." Ethan's voice rumbled softly against her ear. And then he lifted his head and gave her a quizzical, teasing look. "Aren't you the least bit curious to know what the response was to your paintings last night?"

"What paintings?" she murmured dreamily, while her fingers traced an invisible pattern of suggestive hieroglyphics all the way down his spine. And then she realized what he was talking about. "Oh! My paintings! What happened?"

"Not much, except that most of them were marked 'sold' by the end of the evening—and don't you dare think for one second that I had anything to do with it!" he added. "And then there was the well-known art critic who was heard to remark that your work showed 'superb, dramatic use of color' and 'exciting freshness of vision.' So, Jess Winslow, I think your career is about to take off like a rocket—I just hope you'll have time for our honeymoon."

"Mmm, I think I'll manage to schedule it in somehow," she said with a grin, reaching up to tug his sweater over his head, and then letting her hands flutter slowly through his hair and along the back of his neck.

"Why do I get the distinct impression you're not in the mood for talking?" he asked, carefully unfastening her top and bending his head to press a network of hot, wet kisses against her naked white shoulder.

"Whatever gave you the first clue?" she responded breathlessly as Ethan's hands coasted down the sleek curves of her hips and thighs, arousing a rippling, surging tide of sensation within her.

"Oh, well, I wasn't really in the mood for fish chowder tonight, anyway," he said philosophically.

"Fish chowder? *Oh, Lord*—the *chowder!* It must be stuck to the bottom of the pan by now!"

"Well, no." Ethan looked a trifle embarrassed. "Actually, it's just sitting there. I turned the stove off just in case our conversation took a bit longer than you'd planned."

"I always said you were a sneaky man, Ethan Jamieson," Jess said admiringly. "But you're also very wise. Because it just so happens that this particular conversation is going to take a very long time indeed."

"Is that a promise?" Ethan drawled, and his smile sent a warm, liquid sensation of love percolating all through her body.

"Definitely," she whispered as she reached up to ease his shirt off his shoulders and let it slide to the floor. "In fact it might just take us the whole night."

And in fact it did.

THE EDITOR'S CORNER

Imagine the dark night sky on the Fourth of July with myriad fireworks going off—exciting skyrockets buzzing through the air, and wheels of dazzling colors exploding in the dark heavens. We've tried to give you a LOVESWEPT celebration for Independence Day that matches those fireworks in exciting and beautiful reading entertainment.

To start our July "display" we have another real dazzler from Sandra Brown in LOVESWEPT #51, **SEND NO FLOWERS.** As always, Sandra gives us a wonderfully satisfying love story. Do you remember the dear, clinging Alicia from **BREAKFAST IN BED,** LOVESWEPT #22? She was the lady who inadvertently caused the torment that kept Sloan and Carter apart. Well, now Sandra has had Alicia grow up and become an independent woman and an excellent mother for her two boys. Still, though, love has eluded Alicia. But, in **SEND NO FLOWERS,** Alicia meets the man she's never even dared to dream of finding. Alicia has taken her sons on a camping trip when a violent thunderstorm blows up. Just what a mother alone needs, right? Then the devastatingly attractive and gently caring Pierce Reynolds charges to the rescue. Just what a mother alone needs, for sure! Pierce not only saves the family's camping trip, but brings a completeness to Alicia's life that she has never known before. Pierce has a terrible secret, though, and it threatens his and Alicia's new found love. The conclusion of this shimmeringly sensual love story is so highly dramatic and emotionally touching that I suspect you will long remember **SEND NO FLOWERS.**

(continued)

Isn't it interesting to read a love story that's the product of a collaboration between a happily married husband and wife? Think back to **LIGHTNING THAT LINGERS** by Sharon and Tom Curtis, for example. I trust you'll find a special quality of romance in Liv and Ken Harper's first romance for us, **CASEY'S CAVALIER**, LOVESWEPT #52. In this charming book, heroine Casey O'Neil pulls every trick in the book to evade process server Michael Cooper . . . even to faking a heart attack and donning clever disguises. She'll stop at nothing to keep from appearing in court. But nowhere has there ever been a more determined (or heroic!) pursuer than Michael. (He's quite a determined wooer, too!) Casey's and Michael's zany pursuit toward love is like a string of firecrackers going off in this fast-paced love story. You've read the romances by Liv and Ken under the pseudonyms of Jolene Adams (SECOND CHANCE AT LOVE) and JoAnna Brandon (ECSTASY) and now you can enjoy **CASEY'S CAVALIER** published at last under their real names.

You've heard me say it before, but it bears repeating: it's an enormous pleasure for editors to find a brand-new writing talent and publish an author for the very first time. Making her debut as a published author next month is Barbara Boswell with LOVESWEPT #53, **LITTLE CONSEQUENCES**. In this delectable romance Shay Flynn knows that blueblood lawyer Adam Wickwire would make a perfect father for the baby she longs to have . . . but marriage is out of the question—for poignant reasons. So, she makes up her mind to seduce Adam, then vanish forever from his life. When the weekend they spend together leaves her breathless—and more than a little in love—Shay discovers that her perfect plan has resulted in some very, very interesting **LITTLE CONSEQUENCES!** (#53)

A month with a romance by Joan Domning is a month with an extra ray of sunshine! In LOVESWEPT #54, **THE GYPSY AND THE YACHTSMAN,** Joan has outdone herself once more. When heroine Tanya Stanchek's horoscope predicts that "romance will crash into you," she hasn't a clue it's going to happen ... literally! Then a speeding car smacks into hers and tosses the ruggedly handsome Gene Crandall into her path. But a charmingly offbeat fortuneteller, Madame Delores, a mysterious yachtsman whom Tanya has only glimpsed from afar, Gene's biases, and her own anxieties jeopardize the "destined" romance of these two wonderful people. Joan has brewed a delicious stew, seasoned with just the right spices and lots of touching emotion, and I'll bet you agree with me that this is one of her most creative "recipes" for love!

Have a wonderful month of lazy, happy July days brightened up even more by our LOVESWEPT "fireworks."

Warm regards,

Carolyn Nichols

Carolyn Nichols
  Editor
LOVESWEPT
Bantam Books, Inc.
666 Fifth Avenue
New York, NY 10103